MURDER IN CUBA

A Cedar Bay Cozy Mystery - Book 8

BY

DIANNE HARMAN

Published by: Dianne Harman
www.dianneharman.com

Interior, cover design and website by
Vivek Rajan Vivek
www.vivekrajanvivek.com

This is a work of fiction. Names, characters, places, and incidents either are the product of the author's imagination or are used fictitiously, and any resemblance to actual persons, living or dead, business establishments, events, or locales, is entirely coincidental.

ISBN: 978-1522869252

CONTENTS

ACKNOWLEDGMENTS

As always, I thank you my readers, for making my books so popular. I am very indebted to each and every one of you.

My husband and I were fortunate to be asked by Jack Trout to go with him on a fly fishing trip to Cuba. Yes, there really is a real life Jack Trout and a Carola Trout. Our destination in Cuba was Cayo Largo, a small beautiful island off the south coast of Cuba. We spent a week in Cuba and from what my husband tells me, the fly fishing was spectacular. I passed on the fishing, as I preferred to spend my time looking out at the Caribbean Sea and writing this book. The plot is fiction as are all of the characters with the exception of Jack and Carola. Without them, this book never would have been written. I didn't even know that Cayo Largo existed. Let me assure you that my husband is not Mike, and I'm not Kelly, however some of the things in the book are based on actual events such as eating 2 ½ pound lobster tails on the beach and watching a dolphin show.

The idea for the plot began when I saw a door at the local fishing club with three different fish painted on it. Turns out if all three are caught on the same day, the lucky fisherman is eligible to become a member of the Grand Slam Club. My active imagination took it from there. I had a wonderful time writing this book, and the entire Cuban experience was a once-in-a-lifetime experience. Jack and Carola are now taking people to Cuba, and you could be one of them! They can be reached through his website at jacktrout.com.

As always, my thanks to Vivek for the cover of the book, formatting the manuscript, and his pearls of wisdom, and to my husband, Tom, for making my journey through life such a wonderful and rewarding one. Thanks, gentlemen!

Amazing Ebooks & Paperbacks for FREE

Go to www.dianneharman.com/freepaperback.html and get your FREE copies of Dianne's books and Dianne's favorite recipes immediately by signing up for her newsletter.

Once you've signed up for her newsletter you're eligible to win autographed paperbacks. One lucky winner is picked every week. Hurry before the offer ends.

PROLOGUE

Cuba, the land of classic cars, beautiful beaches, salsa music, and the best cigars in the world. There is only one problem - Americans are not allowed to travel directly to Cuba unless they are part of a group that has a legitimate reason for going to the island, such as being part of a cultural exchange group. Individual Americans can't travel to Cuba simply to see the sights, sit on a beautiful sand beach, or enjoy the terrific fishing available in Cuba. But the times they are a changing!

In 2015 the United States resumed diplomatic relations with Cuba some fifty years after an economic embargo on that country had been ordered by President Kennedy. Embassies were established, and a business development frenzy began shortly thereafter. Entrepreneurs of every persuasion saw the abundant opportunities that were on the horizon in Cuba and scrambled to make decisions about how they could be the first in line when Americans were able to once again freely travel to Cuba.

The recreational fly fishing industry was one industry that quickly saw what the future of a Cuba that was open and accessible to Americans might mean. Cuba had always been the Holy Grail for those who loved to fly fish in the tropical waters of the Caribbean nation for bonefish, permit, tarpon, snook, red snapper, and jack trevali. Cuba is home to hundreds of square miles of shallow saltwater ocean flats where these types of fish are commonly found, and for the past fifty years very few American anglers have had an opportunity to fish those waters.

Jack Trout, a well-known fly fishing guide from Northern California is invited to Cayo Largo by Bartolo Fishing Adventures, an Italian company that has a contract with the Cuban government granting them the exclusive rights to fish in the protected areas adjacent to that small Cuban island. The company is anxious to have Jack come to Cuba so he can see for himself the world class fly fishing that is available at Cayo Largo. More importantly, Bartolo extended the invitation to Jack in the hopes that he might consider becoming Bartolo's exclusive representative in the United States. As such, he would be responsible for organizing fly fishing excursions for Americans that want to go fly fishing in Cuba.

Jack calls his good friend, Beaver County, Oregon, Sheriff Mike Reynolds and asks him what he thinks. Mike tells him he's being offered the opportunity of a lifetime, and he definitely should go there and see if it's something he'd be interested in doing. Jack tells him he's already accepted Bartolo's invitation, and he and his wife, Carola, will be traveling there in a month. He asks Mike if he'd be interested in joining them on the trip. Mike quickly replies that he and his wife, Kelly, would be happy to accompany Jack and Carola on their maiden trip to Cuba. He told Jack that Kelly wasn't interested in fishing, and he hoped that would be okay. Jack replied that his wife wasn't either, so he and Mike would do the fishing for them.

Who knew the fishing trip of a lifetime would result in murder? A murder that appeared to be caused by greed, but was that the reason the well-known English fishing guide was killed? Who killed him? The Englishman who is the head of one of the largest international banks in the world? The American with no visible means of support, but has plenty of money to fish all around the world? One of the Cuban fishing guides that worked at Cayo Largo? Or was it Jack?

CHAPTER ONE

"Stay here and watch our luggage. I'll go find the taxi that's supposed to pick us up and take us to the hotel. Jack, you speak a little Spanish. Give me a hand," Carola said. Jack Trout and his beautiful dark-haired Chilean wife walked out into the sweltering late afternoon heat at the Havana airport while Mike and Kelly stood enchanted by the scene unfolding in front of them. Neither of them spoke Spanish, and they were experiencing cultural overload with the sights they were seeing. They were tired and sleep-deprived after their long trip from Oregon, but looking forward to the days they would be spending in Cuba.

Everywhere they looked people were talking excitedly and gesturing. In front of them, just beyond the front doors of the Havana airport, was a never-ending line of classic cars from the 1940's and 1950's. Old Chevrolets, Fords, and Pontiacs that were brightly painted and now being used as taxi cabs vied for cab fares along with the more traditional yellow taxis.

"Mike, I feel like I'm watching a time warp movie. I can't believe I'm really in Havana, Cuba. I've never known anyone who's been here. I remember my parents talking about it, and how just after I was born it became a Communist country and Americans and American products were no longer allowed in the country. I can't wait to try the food. I've read a little about it, and I know they have a lot of fresh seafood," Kelly said.

"I know what you mean. I'm so glad we have Jack and Carola to take care of the language barrier. I don't think we would have made the flight from Mexico City to Havana if it hadn't been for them. It seems like it was one endless line after another. I wouldn't recommend the drive to Portland, the flight to Mexico City, the zoo that was Immigration, and then that wild taxi ride to our hotel to anyone. Our driver had to have been a kamikaze pilot in another lifetime. I'll be honest. I was very, very happy to meet up with Jack and Carola at the Mexico City hotel this morning and let them take over."

"Okay, follow me," Jack said. "Carola found our taxi driver. He didn't think we would clear Customs and Immigration as fast as we did. He was just getting a sign out of his taxi with our names on it when she spotted him."

Jack was quite tall and his wife, Carola, was very petite. They made a fascinating looking couple. They'd been married for a number of years, and she handled all of the business aspects of his international fly fishing guide business, so shepherding people around in a foreign country came quite naturally to her. Her bright red sleeveless tank top and short black skirt made her look like one of the locals. Jack smiled fondly at her as the four of them walked over to the taxi.

"*Buenas dias*," the smiling taxi driver said. "Welcome to Havana." He spoke to Carola in Spanish, and they both laughed.

She turned to Kelly and Mike and said, "Our driver said that's the extent of his English. I'll translate for him on the way to our hotel." A few minutes later, luggage securely in place, they started off. The drive to their hotel was a collage of brightly colored buildings and foliage, along with seeing one classic car after another. Jack and the driver commented about the old classic cars continuously while Mike put in a word occasionally when he knew the make and year of a particular car. Kelly gazed out the window at the nearby Caribbean Sea which they drove beside for several miles, the beautiful old capitol, and the huge cathedral on the way to their hotel. She felt like she'd come one hundred eighty degrees from the overcast forest greenery of the Oregon coast that was their home in the small town of Cedar Bay.

A half hour later the driver stopped in front of a beautiful old hotel that looked like it had been built in the early 20th century. As they walked into the hotel Kelly whispered to Mike, "I feel like I've seen this in a movie. It's Art Nouveau at its best. Look at those bronze statues and this marble floor. Wow!"

Carola stepped up to the reception desk and started checking in for them. A few minutes later she asked the others for their passports and gave them to the reception clerk. She spoke with the clerk, and Kelly and Mike noticed that Jack was grimacing.

"What's wrong?" Mike asked.

"Hate to tell you this, but the van is coming to the hotel tomorrow morning to pick us up at 4:00 a.m. Sorry, but there are very few planes that fly to Cayo Largo. We'll sleep when we get there. Here's your room information. Go on up and get settled. Let's meet at the rooftop restaurant in an hour, have one of their special rum drinks called a mojito, get something to eat, and then call it a night. The receptionist said the view from the rooftop at sunset is spectacular. As long as we're here we might as well try it. By the way, since this is my first trip to Cuba, and its sort of an exploratory trip, my feeling is if someone really recommends something, we need to try it. That way I can decide if it's important enough to do for future clients. I'm going to write several articles for fishing magazines, and I can use the information I gather plus any photographs I take in them."

CHAPTER TWO

Mike inserted the keycard for room 440 in the lock and stepped inside the room. Kelly followed him and exclaimed, "Mike, I have no idea what this cost, but it's incredible. I mean, look at the mahogany furniture in the living room. I can't believe we have a living room with a half-bath off of it, and look, here's another room with a big screen TV, a table for doing business..." Kelly stopped mid-sentence as she walked into the bedroom. "I have never stayed in a room this elegant, and look at this master bathroom. It has everything you'd ever need if you forgot to bring something."

"I wonder what the nightly rate is on something like this, and Kelly, this is not a room, this is a suite. The company who's looking at becoming partners with Jack arranged for everything. I just paid a flat amount for the two of us to come on the trip, but I agree, this is beyond any hotel room I've ever seen. I really feel like I've stepped back a century or more. And did you see that sweeping staircase when we walked into the lobby? I felt like I was Rhett Butler and you were Scarlett O'Hara. Let's do a little unpacking and then go meet Jack and Carola at the restaurant up on the rooftop.

"By the way, from now on I'd feel better if you wore your money belt. I'm putting mine on. It's one thing to hold the carry-ons we had when we were on the plane and last night, but there's no reason to carry all that stuff around with us. What with the cameras, the iPads, the iPhones, and all the other paraphernalia we have in our bags, they're way too heavy. Just put your passport, your credit cards, and your money in your money belt, and we'll leave everything else here."

"Mike, this is only the second time I've been out of the United States, but I've got to tell you how safe I feel with you," she said to the big burly greying middle-aged man. "I mean, I know I'm fairly tall for a woman, and certainly not a lightweight, but one look at you and with the air of authority you carry, no one is going to try and mess with either of us."

"Appreciate your confidence, sweetheart, but don't think that has much to do with it. I'm always concerned in large urban cities. They tend to attract people who would love to charm a beautiful dark-haired woman like you, and as trusting as you are, you'd probably believe what they said only to find out later the person had taken your passport, money or whatever. I heard a horror story once about a guy whose wife was in a wheelchair. He was maneuvering his wife in her wheelchair down a steel ramp in an airport when a man walked by, reached into his pocket, took his wallet, and then said thanks as he walked away. The guy couldn't let go of the wheelchair because his wife would have been injured."

"That's horrible! I did take your advice, and I left my jewelry at home. I'm not even wearing my wedding ring. For all anyone knows, we're just two people who met and decided to spend the night together."

"Well, it might make the next few days very interesting if we pretend were like two strangers meeting in the night," Mike said with a grin. "I kind of like the idea. Well, beautiful lady I've just met, would you join me on the rooftop for the drink your daughter said we had to try in Cuba, a mojito? And don't forget she wants us to text her a picture of it."

"It would be a pleasure and who knows, I might even get to like you enough that you just might get lucky tonight."

"Yeah, as tired as both of us are, in my dreams," he said, holding the door open for her.

*****

They stepped out of the elevator and walked over to the table where Jack and Carola were sitting. Kelly pulled a chair out from the table and exclaimed, "I feel like I'm in a living painting, but I don't think any artist could capture the colors of this sky."

"Don't sit down yet, Kelly, the waiter said this was the perfect time to see the view from the cupola. I waited for you. Come on, it's over this way," Carola said.

They walked past the small band that was just beginning to play their nightly music and stepped up into the cupola. Large openings in the round room allowed a panoramic view of the city, the Caribbean Sea, the capitol, and the mass of humanity below them.

"Carola, thank you so much for everything you've done today. Mike and I would never have been able to do this without you, and if we'd tried, we probably would have had nervous breakdowns. And our room is spectacular."

Kelly noticed that Carola had a funny look on her face and then she said, "I'm glad you like it. Jack was so grateful to Mike for coming with him on this trip that he wanted you to have the special suite, and I couldn't have agreed more."

"Wait a minute," Kelly said, "Are you saying you and Jack don't have the same type of room that we have?"

"No, we were supposed to stay in the suite because the company Jack's working with books their clients at this hotel and evidently they arrange to have the person who is in charge of the group stay in the suite. We have a lovely room, and believe me, I'm not complaining. Now we need to get you a mojito, and I've already ordered lobster tails for all of us. I saw some at the table next to ours, and they looked spectacular."

As they walked down the steps of the cupola Kelly said, "I'm embarrassed you did that for us, but thank you very much. I just wish we were staying longer. That suite definitely does not qualify as a crash pad."

Carola laughed. "Maybe that will help you forget the unconscionable hour you're going to have to get up in the morning. The receptionist told me they'll have sweet rolls and coffee for us at 3:30 tomorrow morning."

When they returned to the table Mike and Jack were deep in a conversation with an American man who appeared to be in his early forties. "Carola, Kelly, I'd like you to meet Philip Montgomery," Jack said. "He's going to be staying at the resort where we'll be for the coming week and fishing with the company we're fishing with, so we'll be seeing a lot of each other for the next week."

Kelly and Carola shook hands with Philip as the bartender arrived with the hotel's signature drink which is also one of Cuba's most popular drinks, mojitos served in a tall glass with a stalk of spearmint muddled in it. Made with rum, they're a staple in Cuba and have recently become very popular in the United States.

"I don't think that's an authentic mojito. It's been my experience that if it doesn't take the bartender at least fifteen minutes to make the drink, it's not being prepared correctly," Philip said arrogantly.

"I wouldn't know about that," Kelly said, "but it sure tastes good. Philip, I detect an accent I can't place. Where are you from?"

"I live in the Florida Keys. I recently moved there from Australia, and when I heard there was a remote Cuban island called Cayo Largo, which means Key Largo in English, I had to come and see what it was like. We have an island in the Florida Keys called Key Largo, and I wanted to see what the differences were between the two islands that share the same name. From everything I've learned about it, the fishing is supposed to be fantastic at Cayo Largo, and I live to fish.

"I also wanted to meet Jack. When I talked to the company who sponsors these trips, I mentioned I'd just started a fishing guide business in Florida, and I told them I would be interested in guiding for them here in Cuba if they were looking for American guides. That's when they told me they had invited a man from Northern California by the name of Jack Trout to see if he'd be interested in working with them. They suggested I talk to Jack. I had a business in Australia, but my wife is from Connecticut, and when our son was born, she insisted we move back to be near her parents. I really didn't want to return to the States, but here I am. Actually, it's kind of nice to get some time away from my wife and at the same time have an opportunity to do some quality fly fishing at Cayo Largo," he said.

Out of the corner of her eye Kelly noticed Carola giving Jack a look that more or less said, "If I have anything to say about it, and I do, this man will never work with or for you."

Jack changed the subject and said, "See the people at the table over there and the guy at the head of the table wearing glasses and a blue fishing shirt? His name is Dudley Samms, and he's a fly fishing guide who caters to English and German fishermen. He's quite well known in Europe, and I've read about him in several fishing magazines. He's brought a fairly large group with him. Looks like about twenty people." Jack laughed and said, "Matter of fact, I recently read he was interested in adding American clients to his list of those who want to fish at Cayo Largo. Seems like there are a lot of people interested in developing this type of business."

He was interrupted by two waiters bringing them plates of lobster tails. The meat had been extracted from the shells and then attractively placed back in them for effect. No one spoke for several minutes while they ate. When Jack was finished, he stood up and said, "I'm going over and introduce myself to Dudley. Since he'll be on the flight to Cayo Largo with us tomorrow, I think I should meet him."

A few minutes later he came back to the table. "Well, Jack, what do you think of him?" Carola asked.

"I feel like a gauntlet has been thrown down. His words to me after I introduced myself and put out my hand were, 'It's always nice to meet my competition for the new business that will be coming from the United States, but from what I hear, I don't think you're going to be much competition. Thanks for coming over, and I'll be seeing you.' He never shook my hand, and he turned back to his group, leaving me standing there like I wasn't even there. I don't think I've ever had anyone be so rude to me. Wow! Wonder if he's that way with his clients?"

"How dare he?" Carola hissed, a caricature at the moment of a hot-blooded South American woman. "You're the best fly fishing guide in the United States. You take people to Chile, British Columbia, Argentina, and all over the United States. Your clients love you, they always catch lots of fish, and a large percentage of them are repeat clients. Sounds to me like he's really scared of you as well he should be."

"Looks like there's going to be some healthy competition for the right to bring Americans to Cuba to go fly fishing at Cayo Largo," Philip said, standing up. "I've enjoyed talking to you. It's going to be a short night and since there are bound to be some Cuban beauties on Cayo Largo, and my wife's not with me, I better get some sleep, so I'll be rested and ready to party with them. See you in the morning. By the way, I was right. That was a lousy mojito." He put some Cuban pesos on the table for his drink and the lobster and walked down the stairs at the far end of the outdoor dining area.

The four of them were quiet for a few minutes, digesting what had taken place. Mike was the first to speak, "Jack, watch your back while you're down here in Cuba. Been my experience when there's money to be made a lot of people are willing to do anything to get it. Don't want you to become a statistic."

Jack laughed. "Sheriff, leave your law enforcement experience at home. This is a fishing trip, not one of your whodunits. I'll be fine."

Later, Jack wished he'd paid more attention to Mike's prophetic words.

CHAPTER THREE

They met in the lobby at 3:30 the next morning. Philip and Dudley's group were already there, drinking coffee and eating sweet rolls. Philip walked over to each person in Dudley's group, introduced himself, and handed them a business card. One of the men looked at it and dropped it on the floor.

"What do you suppose Philip's doing? I can't imagine Dudley would be very happy with whatever it is. I'd love to know what's on his business card," Jack said.

"I need some more coffee, let me see if I can find out," Kelly said. She walked by the table where the man had dropped the card, stooped down, and picked it up. She turned towards the people sitting at the table and said, "Looks like someone dropped this card."

She held it in her hand, but no one claimed it. She stuck it in her pocket and refilled her coffee. When she returned to the table where Jack, Carola, and Mike were sitting she handed it to Jack and said, "Here it is. I didn't have time to look at it. What does it say?"

Jack read it and looked up. "This is pretty amazing. It's got his name, telephone number, the name of his company, and then at the very bottom in bold type it reads 'You Deserve the Best Cuban Fishing Guide. If You Book Any Other Guide, You're Getting One That's Second Rate!' This guy must be on some kind of an ego trip considering the company that arranged this trip told me they want to deal exclusively with me. I don't think they're negotiating with anyone else at the moment."

"I have a really bad feeling about that guy, Jack," Carola said, "I don't want you to have anything to do with him. Over my dead body he'll ever work for you."

"You don't need to worry, Carola. I don't think any of Dudley's group will be interested in him either. If he was any good I think he would have developed a following in Australia, but that doesn't seem to be the case. I've never seen his name advertised in any of the fishing magazines or newspapers. I'll bet he bombed out down there, and now he's trying to tap into the American market. I don't think we're going to have much, if any, Internet service when we get to Cayo Largo, but if we do, Carola, would you see if you can find out anything about him?"

"Sure. Look, a bus just drove up, and everybody's heading toward the front door, pulling their suitcases. Jack, want me to help carry the fly rods? We've done well getting everything here so far, and I'd hate for something to happen on the last leg of our flights to Cayo Largo."

"No. I'm fine. Take your luggage out to where they're loading it on the bus, and I'll make sure it gets on. Go get us a comfortable seat. See you in a few minutes."

*****

They drove through the dark streets of Havana at 4:00 that morning with the streetlights being their only frames of reference. "Mike, I've never seen anything like this. Look at all these people out at this time of night, or should I say early morning? Wonder what's going on," she said as they drove by what looked like a large park.

"Hate to shatter any illusions you have, sweetheart, but I think you may be looking at proof that the oldest profession in the world is alive and well here in Havana. Too many attractive young women in skirts too short to be making their way to jobs in the downtown business district."

"Do you really think that's what's happening?"

"It's not something you see in Cedar Bay, but yes, I definitely think that's what's happening. And from the lack of any law enforcement personnel around, I'd say it is simply a case of willing buyer meets willing seller."

"Well, this is a first for me. I haven't seen anything like that before."

"Look at it this way. We're really in unchartered territory. We've never seen a city like Havana or its airport, and we've never been on a flight at this ungodly hour. Everything is new to us."

After stopping at numerous hotels in Havana and picking up more passengers who were bound for Cayo Largo, the bus pulled into the parking lot of a small regional airport. It was still pitch dark, and once again they had to go through Immigration and security. The security guard made Kelly take her curling iron out of her large carry-on and said something Kelly couldn't understand. Fortunately Carola was directly behind her and told Kelly she'd have to go through the door marked "Private" and put the curling iron in her checked suitcase. After a long wait in the hot and stuffy waiting area, they boarded the plane to Cayo Largo and took off just as dawn was breaking. The gold and light blue colors of the morning sky shined on the scattered puffy white clouds below them. Kelly looked out the window at the blue-green ocean beneath the plane and saw numerous tiny uninhabited islands scattered like little mounds of chocolate in the vast blue sea. She'd read that over 350 small islands comprised the archipelago of which Cayo Largo was a part.

After a short forty minute flight, the plane began its descent, and Kelly saw several large oceanfront hotels facing the bright blue Caribbean. A few minutes later they stepped off the plane and instantly became wet with perspiration caused by the high heat and humidity. As they walked across the tarmac to the small airport building, Kelly thought she heard the sounds of salsa music coming from the building.

I've only been here a few minutes, and already I must be hallucinating. Maybe it's the heat and the humidity. There is no way anyone could be playing salsa music at this hour of the morning. I mean, who would have the energy?

She followed the other passengers into the building and realized the music hadn't been her imagination. At the far end of the building a Cuban couple was dancing to the salsa music accompanied by three musicians.

"Mike, can you believe it? They're really good. I've always wished I could dance like that."

"Tell you what," Carola said. "I'll do it for you. I grew up with this kind of music, and every time I go back home to Chile, we salsa dance." She put down her carry-on luggage and walked over to the couple. Every eye in the airport was riveted on the beautiful small Chilean woman wearing a bright turquoise tube top and short white skirt, sandals tossed off, and looking like a local resident as she started dancing with the Cuban man. The Cuban woman stopped dancing and walked over to the musicians, allowing Carola to take her place. Carola and the man danced until the sounds of luggage being placed on the baggage carousel were heard.

"You were wonderful," Kelly said to Carola. "That was so much fun to watch."

"Sure was," a voice said behind them. Kelly turned and saw Philip standing there. "Carola, I'd sure like you to teach me how to dance like that. I'd even pay you, so I could get that close to you."

Carola looked at him coldly and said, "No thanks." She turned and walked away.

Jack heard the interchange and said, "Little harsh, weren't you, Carola. Maybe the poor guy just wants to learn how to dance salsa."

"Sorry, Jack. That man is not someone I want anything to do with. And I sure as heck don't want to be close enough to him to dance. He makes my skin crawl. The mere thought of being that close to him makes me want to retch," she said as she walked out the door and stood next to the bus that was waiting to take them to their hotel.

Kelly was standing nearby and had watched and heard the interchange between Carola and Philip. She turned to Mike and said, "I don't trust Philip. When Carola turned him down on his offer to pay her for teaching him how to salsa dance he gave her a downright murderous look. Don't think he's used to being turned down much."

"Yeah, I noticed it too. I'll keep an eye out for him. My internal radar kind of goes on high alert when he's around. Come on, time to get to the resort for our next adventure, and right now I'm ready for a sleep adventure, although at this early hour I doubt if our room will be ready."

After a short drive from the airport the bus pulled up to a large yellow and white resort which had numerous detached two story housing units for guests scattered around the five acre complex. Check-in consisted of showing their passports to the clerk, signing a form, and being told that their rooms would be ready in about two hours. They were invited to have breakfast at the open-air buffet restaurant that was next to the lobby. Kelly and Mike counted the minutes until they could go to their room and take a nap. The head guide of the fishing group that had invited Jack to Cuba, Bartolo Fishing Adventures, told Jack he would pick Mike and Jack up at 3:00 that afternoon for an orientation at the nearby fishing club.

CHAPTER FOUR

When their room was ready Kelly and Mike had a bellboy drive them in a golf cart to the building where it was located. It was on the second floor with floor to ceiling windows looking out at the Caribbean and the beach. The blue and white room reflected the blue color of the Caribbean and the sparkling white sand beach. They looked approvingly around at the room they would call home for the coming days and thought it was perfect for their needs.

A few hours later, Kelly and Mike woke up from their naps, put on shorts and gauzy shirts, and headed for the reception area to meet Jack and then go to the fishing club for an orientation on how the fishing for the upcoming days was going to be managed. Kelly had never liked to fish, but she was curious about why Cayo Largo was considered to be a fisherman's paradise. She decided to go with Jack and Mike to the orientation, plus she wanted to know what the plans were.

Bartolo Fishing Adventures maintained a small clubhouse at the nearby marina that was used by their fishermen clients to refresh themselves before and after they went fishing. Beer, water, snacks, and a bathroom were available. The clubhouse walls were covered with photos of successful fishermen holding their catch.

Guido, the head fishing guide, and one of his guides spent the next hour telling Mike and Jack what to expect for the next few days and showing them maps of where they would be fishing and what kind of fish they would be targeting. Guido explained they would be fishing out of sixteen foot outboard motor boats equipped with a 70 horsepower motor. Each boat would have two fishermen, however only one person could fish at a time. He told them that after a fast trip to the nearby saltwater flats the guide turns the motor off and then stands on a small metal four foot high platform mounted at the rear of the boat. While standing on the raised platform the guide is able to quietly move the boat by pushing it with a long twenty-five foot plastic pole.

"The fish you are trying to catch are quite skittish and spook very easily," Guido said. "That's why it's important to quietly pole the boat until you are within easy casting distance. The water on the salt flats is only two to three feet deep and it is quite clear, which makes it easy for the guide to spot the location of the fish. A good experienced guide can pole the boat so quietly you can often get to within ten to twenty feet of the fish, and it will never hear you."

At the end of the one hour orientation they were given special flies they could use for their catch and release fishing. They also received instructions on how to cast and a walk-through of the protocol they were to follow while fishing from the boat. As they were walking back from the dock where the boats were tied up, Kelly spotted a door with three brightly colored fish painted on it surrounded by brilliantly blooming purple bougainvillea plants. "Excuse me, could you tell me what the meaning is of the words on that door?" Kelly asked Guido.

"*Si, senora,*" the handsome Cuban man said. "The words on the door, 'Grand Slam Club,' is in reference to an exclusive club, but very few fishermen achieve a grand slam."

"Pardon me for being ignorant, but I have no idea what you're talking about," Kelly said.

"In fishing jargon here on the island a grand slam refers to a fisherman who catches a tarpon, a bonefish, and a permit all on the same day. It allows them to apply for membership in this very

16

exclusive club which is called the Grand Slam Club. Very few people are able to do it."

"Is the clubhouse behind the door with the fish painted on it?" Kelly asked.

"No, there isn't a physical clubhouse anywhere. If someone qualifies, they fill out an application form that asks when and where they caught their fish. Then they're sent a certificate by an international fishing organization. There's also a super grand slam club, but it's even harder to qualify for it. To qualify for the super grand slam the fisherman must catch the three fish I mentioned plus a fish called a snook, all in the same day."

Kelly turned to Mike and Jack who had followed them up to the clubhouse from the dock. "Well, guys, if we're going to come all this way down here to Cuba, might as well see if either one of you, or hopefully both of you, can become members of the Grand Slam Club. Don't know how important it is in the scheme of things, but sure might give you some major bragging rights when you get back home."

"Don't worry, Kelly, I'll do my best to see that Mike qualifies to become a member of the Grand Slam Club," Jack said with a smile on his face.

They were interrupted by the sounds of a taxi arriving along with loud German and English voices. "Sergio, go get the rest of the guides," Guido said. "Sounds like Dudley's group has arrived. Oh, and remember to tell the cab driver to come back at 6:00. Philip insisted on fishing today and being shown where the other groups are going to be fishing."

"Why would Philip want to know that?" Kelly asked. "Where Mike and Jack fish doesn't affect him."

"That's true, but evidently he paid his guide quite a bit extra if he would give him that information. He said he wanted to outfish them. I have no idea why," Guido said.

That's weird, Kelly thought. *I have no idea why that would be important to him unless he wants to try and show the Bartolo Company that he's a better fisherman than Jack, and that he, rather than Jack, would be a better person to have as a business partner.*

Just then Dudley and his noisy group rounded the corner, and he began yelling at Guido in a loud voice for him to get his group some cold beer and that he wanted it immediately. When the guide turned towards the small room that held the refrigerator containing cold water and beer, she saw Guido roll his eyes heavenward.

Don't think I'd want to be a guide if I had to deal with people like Dudley and Philip. Jack and Mike must seem like a slice of heaven if the typical clients are anything like that group and Philip. The next few days should be very interesting.

CHAPTER FIVE

"Have a wonderful time today, and here's hoping you get a grand slam," Kelly said as Mike got ready for his first day of fishing. "Do you have everything you need?"

"Yeah, but I can't find that special chapstick I brought that has a 30 SPF rating. Jack said he'd heard the sun was brutal out on the water, and since we'll be in it all day, he told me I need to cover every part of my body. He even brought a special thing for me to wear that's kind of like a hooded mask we wear under our hats."

"Better you than me. I intend to do nothing more than eat some Cuban food, take a dip in the Caribbean Sea just so I can say I did, and maybe get a massage. See you tonight, love." She gave him a kiss and opened the door for him, since his hands were full of fishing gear.

An hour later the phone rang, and it was Carola asking Kelly to join her for breakfast, if she hadn't already eaten. Kelly told her she'd meet her in the main dining room which served a large breakfast buffet. As soon as she walked into the dining room, she easily spotted the beautiful Chilean woman sitting at a corner table, smiling and waving her over.

"I thought you'd probably like some coffee, so I had the server bring some. I've never had coffee quite like this. It's frothy, and it almost has a chocolate taste. I wondered if the server had misunderstood me and brought hot chocolate instead, but she assures me it's coffee. It's very good, it's just different."

"I couldn't agree more with you," Kelly said after her first sip. "I read a little bit about Cuban food before I came, but I must have missed the section on coffee."

"Jack told me you own a coffee shop in Cedar Bay, Oregon. I thought you might be interested in the food they have here at the hotel. If you try something you like, since you don't speak Spanish, and it's my native tongue, I might be able to get some information about it for you."

"That would be wonderful. I was concerned about how I could get the recipe for a dish if I liked it, given the fact I don't speak Spanish."

"I'd be happy to help you. The people here at the resort seem to be very accommodating. Are you ready to make the rounds of the different food stations?"

"Absolutely. My stomach just woke up and says it has to try something different than what we usually have in the States."

A few minutes later they both sat down, plates laden with sausages, meatballs, different kinds of homemade breads, and a few things that hadn't been labeled. As Kelly picked up her fork she said, "Carola, I understand you handle the business side of Jack's fishing guide business. Tell me what you do, and how a Chilean woman happened to marry a fishing guide from Northern California."

"I met Jack when he was guiding for a group he'd brought to Chile. He'd taken them to a bar for a beer after they'd been out on the river all day. I happened to go there after work with a friend. I worked for a travel company that arranged fishing tours for groups from all over the world. Jack's Spanish was so-so," she said wiggling her flattened hand back and forth. "He was trying to tell the bartender he wanted six very cold beers. He had the word 'cervaza' down, but the very cold part was beyond his limited Spanish.

"I heard him try to order and realized the bartender couldn't figure out what he was saying, so I walked over and told the bartender what he wanted. As they say, the rest is history. He came back to the little town where I lived two more times, and when he got ready to leave with his group the last time he asked me to marry him. We got married in Chile, and I moved to Northern California."

"Wasn't that hard, I mean you must have had a lot of family there."

"Yes, it was very hard, but what works so well is he goes back to Chile several times a year to act as a fishing guide for different groups and naturally, I travel with him, and I get to see my family. I make all of the travel arrangements for the groups that hire Jack, and since Spanish is my first language I can really help when we encounter problems such as a client needing emergency medical attention or whatever. I do the bookwork for his company, but that's really easy, because it's what I did before I met Jack.

"I've helped Jack expand his guiding services to the point where he's now considered to be one of the best fly fishing guides in the United States. I'm lucky I like to travel, because we go all over the world. It's really fun, and most of the people we meet are very nice. Actually, more than fifty percent of our clients are repeat customers. It's fun to keep up with what's happening in their lives and feeling like you're going to spend time with old friends. I love my new life with Jack. He's such a wonderful caring man."

Kelly had been eating the whole time Carola had been talking. "I'm so glad to hear that. Mike told me Jack has never been happier, and I guess he and Jack go way back to a time before either one of them had met either one of us. Let me change the subject. I wonder if there's any way I could get the recipe for these meatballs. I think the sign on them said albondigas in sauce. I'll go look and tell you specifically."

She stood up and walked over to the central hot food station.

She'd brought a piece of paper and a pen with her, so she could write down the names of any dishes that particularly appealed to her. She was writing the specific name of the dish down when she became aware of a conversation taking place behind her. Eavesdropping came as natural to her as eating, and she couldn't resist spending a few moments seemingly writing down the names of several dishes as the two women behind her carried on a conversation.

"I've never heard such a loud and angry argument. They must be English, because Dudley is such an English name. Evidently she'd unpacked for him while he'd gone to the marina for his fishing group's orientation after they'd arrived. From what I could hear, she'd found a receipt for a hotel in London in his suitcase on a date when he told her he'd been off guiding a group of fishermen in Scotland."

"So they were in the room next to you, and you could hear everything they were saying through the wall between the two rooms. What else did they say?"

"She was ranting and raving and screaming at him. She told him that was the final straw, and she'd suspected for a long time he was having an affair. She said she was leaving him when this trip was over, and he'd have to find someone else to pay his bills and support him. Then she told him she was pretty sure she knew who the woman was."

"He told her he hadn't loved her for a long time, and that the only reason he'd stayed with her was because she was wealthy, but here's the part that kind of freaked me out. She yelled at him that he'd better watch it, because he was worth a lot more to her dead than alive, since she wouldn't have to spend any more money on him."

"Wow! Did you call security or anything?"

"No. I mean it would have been my word against theirs, and from what I hear, the English don't usually like to air their dirty laundry out for all to see, if you know what I mean."

"Did you get a chance to see her?"

"Well, I'm not real proud of this, and I probably wouldn't admit it to anyone but you, but I heard the door slam and footsteps going down the stairs. I opened my door ever so slightly, and I saw a woman walking onto the path from the steps. I couldn't see her face, but I saw her blond hair. She was fairly tall and slender. That's all I know."

"I'll definitely be on the lookout for a tall slender woman with blond hair. Since almost all of the people here at the resort are from South America and Europe, there can't be many women who fit that description. I think I'll go over to the omelet station and have them make one for me. Any time there's a line that long I figure it means there's good food. Want to join me?"

"Definitely. I can't let you eat alone," she said laughing.

Kelly walked back to the table and saw Carola smiling broadly at her as she approached.

"Kelly, this is going to be such fun. I was able to make an appointment with the chef during his quiet time this afternoon between lunch and dinner. We're to meet him at 3:30. He doesn't speak English, so I'll have to interpret for you. I see that you brought some paper. Make sure you have plenty for our meeting. You were over there a long time. Did you get the names of some other dishes you're interested in?"

"Yes, but that's not the only information I got. Since Jack wasn't very thrilled with Dudley Samms, let me tell you about a conversation I overheard." She told Carola about the conversation that had evidently taken place between Dudley and his wife the evening before.

"Wow," Carola said. "I remember when we were at the rooftop restaurant in Havana and Dudley was so rude to Jack there was a blond woman sitting at his table. It must have been his wife. Now I'm curious. If I recognize a tall blond woman who looks English, I'll see if I can start a conversation with her about what it's like to be married to a fishing guide."

CHAPTER SIX

After they'd finished eating, Carola said, "Since we won't have time for a swim in the Caribbean this afternoon because of our meeting with the chef, are you game for doing it now?"

"I'm game, but I want you to remember one thing. You're twenty years younger than I am, so please don't comment on my sagging body parts. I'm way past the bikini years."

"Kelly, you look wonderful. Don't sell yourself short, but I do want to remind you that this is a clothing optional beach, and European women seem in some ways to have a much healthier outlook towards aging bodies than American women do. I don't want you to be shocked by anything you might see."

"I promise you I won't embarrass you by pointing or staring, but I have to admit I've never been to a clothing optional beach. Kind of makes me uncomfortable, but then again, I come from the small town of Cedar Bay where if anyone went topless they'd be arrested, and while I think I'm quite open to things, I'd sure as heck hope that the arresting officer wasn't my husband," Kelly said laughing.

Carola smiled as she said, "Meet you in twenty minutes at the stairs that lead to the beach."

*****

"I don't know when I've felt so invigorated," Kelly said as the two women left the water and walked towards the lounge chairs that had been set up on the beach for the resort guests. "The water temperature is so different from the Pacific Ocean in Oregon. It almost feels like the temperature of my skin. I love it that the chaises aren't all piled close together but spaced far enough apart that I feel like the sand and the water are exclusive to us. I'm surprised I don't see any lifeguards. There are lifeguard towers, just no lifeguards."

"I've traveled enough to know that Americans seem hung up on safety. Maybe it's because they're so afraid of being sued. I noticed there aren't any handrails on most of the stairs I've been on, so I can't say I'm particularly surprised there aren't any lifeguards.

"Why don't we meet for lunch in about forty-five minutes? I can hear music coming from the restaurant, so it must be open. Kelly, look, there's a tall slender blond woman walking towards the restaurant. She looks like the woman I saw in Havana. Let's go eat now. I'd like to go over and introduce myself to her. I'm kind of curious about her based on what you overheard. We can shower after lunch and before our meeting with the chef. Would that be okay with you?"

"Yes, I'm just as curious as you are, but she might feel uncomfortable if we both descend on her. Why don't we get a table and see where she's sitting. If it looks like it's a natural thing, you could go over and strike up a conversation with her."

They sat down and Carola told the server in fluent Spanish that they would both like a mojito. Kelly loved to watch Carola speak to the servers. It was like watching a movie. People who spoke the language seemed to use every part of their body when they were speaking. It wasn't just the mouth moving. Arm movements, eye movements, body language, hands gesturing, head nodding - everything accentuated what was being said.

"Carola, you know I don't speak the language, but I thought I

26

heard you say the word 'mojito.' Did you order mojitos for us?"

"Of course. I overheard someone say that the bartender here makes the best mojito in all of Cuba. Since we're here I thought we should try one."

"I don't think I've ever had a drink this early in the day, but what the heck, I'm on vacation. I just hope I don't fall asleep when I'm talking to the chef, or rather when you're talking to him."

"Kelly, the one thing I've learned in all of the traveling I've done with Jack is to do what the locals are doing, and the people here at the resort are drinking mojitos with their lunch. Consider it part of adapting to the culture."

"I'll take your word for it," she said as the server placed a mojito in front of each of them. Kelly looked at it for a moment, picked it up, and said, "*Salud.* I seem to remember that word means health in Spanish or close to it and is used in toasts." She took a sip of her mojito. "Carola, I had my doubts a few moments ago, but this is really delicious. Wouldn't want to serve one at Kelly's Koffee Shop and anyway, I don't have a liquor license, but I definitely am going to enjoy this one."

"Kelly, the woman we think is Dudley's wife is sitting over there in the corner by herself. I'll be back in a few minutes."

*****

"Pardon me, but I believe I saw you in Havana night before last. Aren't you Dudley Samms' wife?" Carola said as she sat down across from the woman.

"Yes, I'm Patricia Samms, and you are?" the woman asked.

"My name is Carola. I'm Jack Trout's wife. I'm always eager to meet the wife of a fishing guide. It seems we have so much in common even if we do live in different parts of the world. Have you been involved in this for very long?"

"I've been married to Dudley for fifteen years, and in many ways it feels like a lifetime. Actually, I don't think Dudley will be in business much longer. It's time he went on to something else."

"Really? Like what?"

"I don't know exactly. I'm not sure anyone does. I hope you'll excuse me," she said standing up. "I really came in here just to get some cold water. I'm going to spend the afternoon at the beach. I love the ocean, and living in England I don't have too many chances to swim in water this warm. It was nice talking to you."

Kelly saw Carola approaching their table and when she sat down she asked, "Well? Did you learn anything?"

"The only thing I learned was that was the weirdest conversation I've ever had. I honestly can't make any sense of it."

"You've definitely aroused my curiosity. What did she say?"

When Carola finished relating the contents of the short conversation she'd had with Patricia Samms, Kelly said, "I agree with you. That sounds like the strangest conversation I've ever heard of too."

They finished eating their lunch and agreed to meet at the restaurant at 3:30. "Kelly, be sure and bring the names of the dishes you're interested in getting the recipes for. I have no idea what the resort's policy is on something like this, but I seem to remember reading that the resort recently hired a famous Cuban chef to update their menu. If the chef brought his own recipes and dishes to the resort, I would think he could share them with you. We'll have to see. Should be interesting. See you later."

CHAPTER SEVEN

Promptly at 3:30 that afternoon Kelly met Carola at the entrance to the restaurant. A young woman walked over to them and asked Carola if they were the women who were meeting with Chef Fuentos. She replied yes, and the young woman indicated they were to follow her. They walked through the empty restaurant, and the woman stopped in front of a door marked "Chef Fuentos." She knocked, and a moment later it was opened by a large Cuban man wearing the traditional chef's uniform consisting of a white toque (a chef's hat), a white double-breasted jacket, and checkered pants. He smiled broadly and said, *"Buenas tardes,"* then he spoke rapidly in Spanish to Carola and closed the door behind them.

Carola turned to Kelly and said, "Chef Fuentos welcomes you and would like to help you as best he can. He speaks almost no English, so I'll be translating for him. What would you like to know?"

"I'm very interested in the history of Cuban food. Could he tell me what some of the influences have been?"

The chef and Carola spoke back and forth for several minutes while Carola took notes and then said, "Rather than translate everything as he's saying it, I think it would be much easier if I sum up what he says."

"I'm fine with however you want to do this. Please, make it as easy as possible for both of you. I just wish I spoke Spanish, so this wouldn't be necessary. I'd like you to thank him again for agreeing to meet with me."

Carola translated what Kelly had said, and the chef smiled broadly as he began to speak in rapid Spanish. A few minutes later Carola said, "Kelly, here's pretty much what he told me about the history of the food. He says it's a blend of several kinds of cuisines including Spanish, since they colonized Cuba, African, because so many Africans were brought to Cuba as slaves, French from the French colonists that came to Cuba from Haiti, and the Native American Tainos."

"Excuse me," Kelly interrupted, "I've never heard of the Tainos. Who were they?"

Another exchange took place between the chef and Carola, and then she said, "They were a tribe in the Caribbean and in Florida. Don't forget that Cuba's only about ninety miles from the tip of Florida, so there has always been a lot of interaction between the two countries."

"Okay, I think I understand the influence these other countries had on Cuban food, and I can certainly see it in some of the dishes. Now please ask him what foods would be considered common in Cuba."

The large affable chef gestured broadly when he was talking, and Kelly wished she had a video camera she could use to record his movements. His dark skin against the white uniform that he wore, his large brown eyes, and a face that was seldom without a smile made him a very appealing subject.

"He says a typical meal usually consists of some rice and beans prepared either together or separately. They have different names based on the method of preparation. The main course would usually be pork or beef, and because Cuba is an island, the Cubans eat a lot of fish and seafood. He said there are a lot of tubers such as yuccas, potatoes, and malangas…"

"Sorry, but I'm completely unfamiliar with malangas. What are they?"

"I don't have to bother him with that, since I know. It's like a potato, just not as common."

"Thanks."

"Plantains are quite common along with tropical fruits, such as mangoes. He said when the embargo started many years ago, and Cubans could no longer get orange juice, mango juice became the common breakfast drink."

"I didn't even think of that, but now I'm curious. Would you ask him how the embargo affected the way Cubans eat?"

Carola asked the chef and made notes as she listened to him. When he was finished she said, "One of the biggest things was that Cuba Libres, the popular drink invented in Cuba, which consists of rum, coke, and lime, and means "Free Cuba," had to be changed, because Cuba could no longer import Coca Cola, since it's made in America. He said Cubans now use a cola made here in Cuba, but personally he doesn't think it's as good as Coca Cola."

"I've never had a Cuba Libre, so I wouldn't know the difference, but I guess the reverse would be true as well. I don't think Cuban rum is imported into the United States, so even in the United States, the drink wouldn't be authentic."

"I've written down a number of other things he says can't be brought into the country from the United States. I'll give the list to you later. I don't want to take too much of his time. What else would you like to know?"

"Thank him for granting us this much time. I'd like to know where he got his training and why he was hired as the chef here at the resort. Lastly there are some recipes I'd like to have that are dishes prepared and served here at the hotel."

Again, Carola and the chef carried on an animated conversation while Kelly watched, fascinated by how much body language and gesticulating each of them used while they were talking.

"He has wealthy relatives in Paris who offered to pay for him to attend the Cordon Bleu Culinary Arts School there and live with them, which he did. He says when he returned to Cuba he worked in a number of restaurants, but they barely paid a living wage. He heard that this hotel was looking for a chef, and he applied for the job. He says he's free to make whatever dishes he chooses, and for a chef, it's probably the best job one could have in Cuba. One of his favorite things is when he gets to prepare special meals for the honeymooners who rent the cabana outside the restaurant for a romantic candlelight dinner."

"Please tell him that the food here is some of the best I've ever eaten. I have five recipes that I would like to have. Tell him I own a coffee shop or a small restaurant in Oregon on the West Coast of the United States. I would love to serve the dishes there, and I would give credit to him for the dishes."

When Carola translated Kelly's request to the chef, he smiled broadly at her and spoke rapidly to Carola. "He wants to know which recipes you want."

Kelly looked at the Spanish names of the dishes she had written down, and said, "I would love to have the recipes for Arroz con Pollo, Arroz con Leche, Albondigas, Moros y Cristianos, and Pastel de Tres Leches. If he could give me these, I would be very happy."

Before Carola could even translate, the chef was smiling and nodding his head, clearly understanding the Spanish names of the dishes Kelly had requested. He spoke to Carola for a moment.

"The chef says to tell you he personally made changes to those five dishes when he became chef, and the ones being served are his creations. He will gladly give you the recipes. The chef says he will tell his assistant to have them copied, and an envelope containing the recipes will be waiting for you at the front desk tomorrow morning.

He said he would do it now, but his assistant is on a break until dinner.

Kelly stood up, smiled broadly, and said, *"Muchas gracias,* Chef Fuentos." Turning to Carola she said, "I think we need to leave. I wish I could say more to him, but hopefully he'll know how much I appreciate his time and information."

Carola spoke to the chef for several more minutes and then walked over to him and kissed him on each cheek. She turned to Kelly and said, "He says he's enjoyed his time with us, and although many people have thanked him for his cooking, no one has ever taken the time away from their vacation activities to ask him the questions you did, and he's honored."

"One last thing," Kelly said, "tell him I'm the one who is honored." She smiled at the chef and walked out of the room, Carola following a moment later.

"Thank you so much, Carola. I am so excited to get those recipes, and I definitely plan on serving them at my coffee shop."

"So what you're saying is that if I get hungry for authentic Cuban food, all I need to do is take a trip to Kelly's Koffee Shop?" she asked mischievously.

"My friend, you are always welcome at the coffee shop or in our home. We'd love to have you."

"Might just take you up on it," Carola answered.

CHAPTER EIGHT

Stewart had been on several fly fishing trips with Dudley to various parts of the world and had told Dudley he would go on this trip under one condition. He would pay Dudley an extra thousand Euros if Dudley would agree to fish with him on the first day and help him catch the three types of fish needed to qualify for the Grand Slam Club. Stewart had told him how he'd read about the Grand Slam Club, and since no Englishman had ever become a member of it, he wanted to be the first to qualify.

The next morning a van picked up Dudley's group, along with Philip, Jack, and Mike, from the hotel at 8:00. They drove the short distance to the marina and divided themselves into groups of two with a guide assigned to each group and prepared to go to the zone assigned to each of the boats. There were five fishermen plus Dudley in his group, Jack and Mike, plus Philip and his guide. Within minutes they'd put on their sun-protection gear and were on the way to their assigned zones. That way one particular area wouldn't be overfished, and it gave each of the fishermen an equal opportunity to qualify for the Grand Slam Club - and with it bragging rights for the rest of the fisherman's life!

"Dudley, remember, I paid you a thousand extra Euros for you to fish with me today so I could catch the tarpon, bonefish, and permit I need to catch to qualify for the Grand Slam Club," Stewart said.

"I will do what I can, but I can't cast for you, and you know that's always been your downfall. Did you listen to the guide explain about casting to the clock? Remember, when he gets us to where he thinks the fish will be, he'll tell you to cast to eleven o'clock, or three, or whatever. Once you have a fish on your line, I'll tell you what to do, but remember, I can't cast for you."

At 12:30 the guide told them it was time to go to a small islet where they'd meet the other boats in their group and have the lunch each of them had packed from the breakfast buffet. Dudley looked at a grim-faced Stewart and said, "Do you have any idea how many fish you could have caught if you'd just learned to cast properly? The chances for qualifying for the Grand Slam Club were all there, but with your casting you couldn't get hooked up to one."

Even though their guide, Stefano, wore sunglasses and a full mask to protect his face from the sun, Stewart could tell he was laughing at him. Dudley didn't even help Stewart out of the boat when the guide eased the boat onto the beach. Dudley shook his head disgustedly when one of his group from another boat asked, "Did your boat have any luck this morning, Dudley?"

"You mean could we have or did we catch anything? We could have caught a lot, but with Stewart's lousy casting it didn't happen, so no, we didn't get anything, and you, any luck?"

"It was a great morning. We each got two bonefish, I got a tarpon, and Christoph caught a permit. We've both got a chance to become the first Englishman to qualify to become a member of the Grand Slam Club."

"Well, good luck. Don't think there will be any competition coming from my boat," Dudley said, nodding his head towards where Stewart had stepped into the bushes to commune with nature. A few moments later Stewart emerged with a sour look on his face. They sat under some pine trees that provided a cushion of soft pine needles on the ground and threw pieces of bread from their sandwiches to the iguanas who had greeted them as soon as they'd come ashore. It was obvious the iguanas had learned to rely on food from fishermen rather than scavenging on their own as their ancestors had done for eons.

Rested, the fishermen and the guides returned to their boats. "Good luck, Stewart, Dudley," Christoph said.

"We'll need it," Dudley replied. Stewart glowered and didn't answer Christoph.

He's the reason I'm not catching any fish, but I need him for the rest of the afternoon, Stewart thought. *He's the best fishing guide in England, and I'm certainly paying him enough to help me. He's ruined my self-confidence. The only thing I've gotten for my money is he let me fish all morning, rather than us taking turns. If he'd gotten the three fish and qualified for the Grand Slam Club I think I would have killed him. I'll see what happens this afternoon.*

Stewart's afternoon went no better than his morning had gone. No matter what number on the face of a clock the guide yelled out as he stood on the tower while he poled the boat, when Stewart cast in that direction, it never resulted in a hook-up. Finally at four that afternoon, Dudley turned to Stewart and said, "That's all. You've had more than enough chances to be the first Englishman to qualify for the Grand Slam Club, and you've blown every one of them. Let me show you what a real fisherman can do. Stefano, get up on that tower and call out the numbers to me."

To Stewart's utter dismay, one hour later Dudley's photograph was being taken with first a tarpon, then with a bonefish, and finally with a permit. Dudley Samms would be the first Englishman to qualify for the Grand Slam Club. When they returned to the marina at 5:15, Stewart watched the other fishermen congratulate Dudley on making English fishing history. All he could think about was how it could have been him if it wasn't for Dudley's voiced and unvoiced criticism of his casting ability. He seethed with anger, knowing his blood pressure was far higher than it should be. He made a mental note to take a couple of blood pressure pills as soon as he got back to his room at the hotel.

CHAPTER NINE

The van ride back to the hotel was even worse. Philip, Mike, and Jack congratulated Dudley on his achievement, and although none of them particularly liked Dudley, they felt duty bound to honor his fishing prowess.

"Thanks," Dudley said. He looked at Jack and Philip and said, "Guess you two can say goodbye to your hopes of becoming the official representative for any United States fly fishermen that want to come to Cuba. When the people at Bartolo hear what I've done today, they're definitely going to want me to be their exclusive representative for booking trips for American fly fishermen. I need to start making plans to open a couple of offices in the United States. Don't want to step on either one of your toes, but the Pacific Northwest and Florida are the natural places for them. The bulk of American fly fishermen come from those areas. I'm thinking maybe I'll pay you a small referral fee for any clients you send me. We'll work out the details once I get the go-ahead from Bartolo."

Mike looked at Jack and couldn't believe what he was hearing. Jack simply smiled and nodded. Out of the corner of his eye Mike noticed that Philip looked really angry. Although his face was red, and his fists were clenched, he didn't say anything.

"I didn't know when I came here it would be so easy to do," Dudley bragged in a loud voice, "I don't know why some other

Englishman hasn't become the first member of the Grand Slam Club. I guess I really am the best fly fisherman in England. Too bad Stewart Bond wasn't first, but if you're not any good at casting, you can't catch fish. Simple as that, right, Stewart?" Stewart stoically stared out the window of the van and refused to answer him.

After the short trip from the marina the van pulled up in front of the resort, and the men carried their equipment into the reception area. Mike had just started to head for his room when he heard Kelly's voice calling to him. "Mike, I'm meeting Carola in the bar. Why don't you join us for a beer before you go to the room? I want to hear all about the day's fishing."

Carola walked up at that moment and said, "So do I. Mike, do you know if Jack already went to our room?"

"Yes. He said he wanted to take a shower and then go for a swim in the ocean before it got dark. He said he'd meet us at the restaurant at eight. Although I could use a shower, a cold beer sounds better at the moment. This heat and humidity is really something."

They walked over to the open-air bar and sat at a table at the back of the room. They chatted casually, filling each other in on the events of the day as they sipped their cold beer. Forty-five minutes later they heard a siren. Mike cocked his ear and said, "If we were in the States, I'd say that was an ambulance, and it seems to be getting closer. I wonder what's going on. Stay here. I'll be back in a minute. I know it's a sheriff thing, but I can't hear a siren without having it arouse my curiosity."

"I wonder what's going on," Kelly said fifteen minutes later. "Mike's been gone for a long time. Stay here, Carola, and hold our seats. I'll see if I can find out what's happening."

She walked down the path that led to the reception area and saw some flashing blue and red lights coming from an ambulance. Mike was standing in front of it talking to the ambulance personnel and a man who looked like he was a policeman. Several hotel employees were there as well. She made her way through the gathering crowd and stood next to Mike as the ambulance attendants put a body covered with a white sheet in the ambulance.

He looked down at her as she asked, "What's happened?"

"It looks like Dudley went for a swim in the ocean and drowned. A couple was taking a twilight walk along the beach and found his body. It must be an incoming tide because his body washed up on shore almost immediately after he died."

"Is there anyone on the island who can determine the cause of his death?"

"No. The island's so small there's no coroner, so they're flying one over from the mainland. The hotel's house doctor did a quick examination of the body and from what the people around me said, he thought Dudley probably had of a heart attack and then drowned. The coroner's coming here in the morning, and he'll do an examination of the body. The hotel doesn't want the slightest hint of any possibility that there was foul play. Looks like my shower will have to wait because the constable wants to talk to the fishermen Dudley was with today to see if anyone can shed some light on the cause of his death. The doctor did say he thought it was very unusual for a man in his early forties to die of a heart attack."

"I'm no expert, but I'd have to agree. That does seem very unusual," Kelly responded.

"Kelly, I haven't had a chance to tell you about it, but Dudley was really belittling Stewart, the guy he fished with today. That's not all. He was acting like a first class jerk. He told Jack and Philip, the guy from Florida, that they could forget about being Bartolo's exclusive representative in the United States, because he was bound to get the position since he was the first English fisherman to qualify for the Grand Slam Club. He even said he was going to open offices in the Pacific Northwest and Florida since that's where most of the Cuban fly fishing business comes from. At the time I thought it was a real insulting slap in the face for both Jack and Philip. Philip looked furious, but Jack, as is typical of him, simply smiled. If it turns out

Dudley didn't die of natural causes, it might be worth taking a look at this guy Stewart. He was practically smoking he was so angry at Dudley."

"Yeah, well I haven't had a chance to tell you about the conversation I overheard about the fight Dudley and his wife had last night as well as the conversation Carola had with her," Kelly said. She related the two conversations to him.

He raised an eyebrow and said, "It will be very interesting what the coroner has to say about the cause of death. If it turns out it was foul play, it looks like there are already a couple of people I'd be inclined to think of as suspects. I suppose Jack would qualify to be one as well since he's interested in getting the Bartolo contract, but I can't believe he'd have anything to do with it. Why don't you go on back in the bar and tell Carola what's happened? Looks like most of the people who were with Dudley today are here now, and the constable is motioning us into a room. I don't see Jack, so I'll give him a call. It shouldn't take too long, but then again I've never been questioned by Cuban authorities. See you in a little while."

"You were sure gone a long time," Carola said when Kelly walked back to the table where she was sitting. "What's happening?"

"This is really quite shocking, but evidently Dudley Samms' body washed up on shore a little while ago. The resort doctor was called and thinks he probably had a heart attack while he was swimming, but he also said Dudley seemed too young to suffer cardiac arrest. Mike told me the coroner is flying to the island tomorrow morning from Havana, which is as soon as he can get here. He told me a few other things that may make it interesting if it's determined Dudley didn't die from natural causes." Kelly went on to tell her what had happened in the van on the way back from the marina.

"Carola, I don't want to alarm you, but you know Mike is the Beaver County, Oregon Sheriff. He's been involved in several murder cases over the last couple of years, and I've helped him as well. I hate to tell you this, but if the coroner finds that Dudley was murdered, Jack could be a suspect, and here's why. Mike says the first place you look when trying to solve a murder case is to find out who has the most to gain from the victim being murdered. "In Dudley's case, from what Mike told me, there could be several people. Certainly Philip and Jack, because now one of their competitors for the Bartolo contract is no longer around. Mike told me he would do whatever was necessary to clear Jack's name if it does turn out to be a case of murder. I just want you to know ahead of time that it's a possibility."

"You've got to be kidding! Jack is the kindest, gentlest person I've ever known. That's why he specializes in catch and release fishing. He can't stand to guide clients he calls 'meat fishers.' You know, the type that want to kill every fish they catch and put it in an ice chest. No, there is absolutely no way my husband could have done something like that. He is simply incapable of it."

"From what Mike's told me about Jack, I would have to agree. Mike said Philip was really mad at Dudley, and he felt Dudley had unfairly embarrassed and demeaned Stewart. Those are two others who could be considered suspects, and then there's his wife."

Mike walked into the bar followed by Jack, just as Kelly finished telling Carola what Mike had told her. Carola stood up and hugged Jack. "Honey, I am so sorry about this. Are you all right?"

"Yes, I'm fine, but obviously Dudley isn't. I told the constable I'd gone for a swim about the time Dudley's body was discovered, but I hadn't seen anything. I hope he believed me."

"You're not the only one. Let's go up to the room. I imagine you could use a little quiet time right now." She turned to Mike and Kelly. "It's 7:00 now. Let's meet in the restaurant at 8:00. Maybe someone will know more then."

"Sounds good," Kelly said. "Mike, I imagine you could use a little rest too after a long hot day in the sun."

They met in the restaurant, but dinner was a somber affair given the recent turn of events. They called it a night as soon as they finished dinner and retired to their rooms.

CHAPTER TEN

The next morning Kelly kissed Mike goodbye and wished him luck as he scurried around the room making sure he had everything he'd need for the day's fishing. She'd had no luck with the coffeepot or hot water pot that was in the room. The only thing she could find next to it was decaffeinated coffee, and she definitely needed something with a kick to begin her morning. After she finished dressing she decided to walk down to the buffet restaurant and get some coffee. It was already sunny and humid and the breeze almost blew the floppy sun hat she was wearing off of her head before she could make it down the steps of their building. When she got to the bottom she thought she heard something.

She looked down to see where the sound had come from and saw a very small cat. She bent down to pet it as it mewed and wrapped itself around her ankles. "Aren't you a little beauty?" she said to the amber and white colored cat. She gently stroked its soft fur and was rewarded with the cat purring. "Who do you belong to, and where do you live, little one?" Although she knew the cat couldn't answer, she couldn't help but ask the question as she looked around but didn't see anyone. "Do you belong to the resort? Are you in charge of making sure there aren't any mice or other things tourists might not like?"

Kelly stood up and said, "Little cat, I think I'll call you Cayo after the name of this island. I have to go now, but I hope to see you again."

The calico cat looked up at her as if to say, "You're definitely going to see me again. Matter of fact I'm going with you. They know me in the restaurant. Let's go." Cayo took a few steps in front of Kelly and then looked back at her as if to say, "Well, are you coming or not?"

"This is something I didn't expect. Guess there's a lot that happens on this island I don't know about. If you want to come with me, you're more than welcome," she said to the little cat. The two of them walked over to the open-air restaurant and entered it. There was no doubt Cayo was quite at home in the restaurant.

Kelly sat down and immediately a server came over to her table, reached down, and petted the small cat while at the same time asking Kelly if she would like some juice or coffee. The cat stretched out under the table as if it belonged there.

"Black coffee, please. It looks like you know this cat."

"Ah, yes. Many people feed him, and he keeps the mice and other little critters in check. We like him very much, but he has never stayed with just one person. Usually he walks through the restaurant hoping to find someone who will give him food. You must own a cat, and he senses you are a friend."

"No, I have two dogs. I've never owned a cat. I really don't know anything about them."

"Animals always know about people. You might not have a cat now but you will. He can tell."

Oh yeah, Kelly thought. *With two dogs, and the last one pretty difficult to get Mike to accept, don't see that happening anytime soon.*

She sipped her coffee and had the same thought that she'd had the morning before about the coffee tasting more like foamy hot chocolate than the black coffee she was used to at home. She'd decided yesterday that it wasn't bad, just different. Meanwhile Cayo snored softly beneath her feet. She pushed her chair back, being careful not to disturb him. She circled around all of the breakfast stations trying to decide what to have for breakfast.

Good grief. I have never seen such a breakfast display. Whatever country you're from, and whatever you're used to eating for breakfast, it's here. I'd like to try everything, but not only would I be in a food coma for the rest of the day, Mike would have to hire a forklift to get me on the plane when it's time to go home. Probably not a good thing to do. She settled for a fresh shrimp omelet and some fruit.

The savory taste of the freshly caught shrimp in the omelet reminded her of what Carola had eaten for dinner the previous night. She'd opted for shrimp pasta with mushrooms, calamari, onions and garlic. It looked so good Kelly had already decided that's what she was going to have for dinner tonight. What fascinated her was Carola's description of how the chef had prepared it. Evidently he'd taken precooked pasta and put it in a cylindrical sieve type container which he plunged into simmering hot water. Carola told him what she wanted in her pasta, and he squeezed oil from a bottle into a pan which was sizzling hot, flash fried the ingredients, and asked Carola what kind of sauce she wanted on her pasta. The choices were bolognese, white, or a combination of the two. He'd taken a ladle of the sauce from a container, mixed it with the sizzling ingredients, drained the pasta, and put it in the sizzling pan. He mixed the ingredients together and plated it. Kelly had looked enviously at the pasta plate, and Carola confirmed it was every bit as good as it looked.

If it's half as good as it looked, I could easily serve that at the coffee shop. I could have a list of ingredients and customize a pasta plate for customers. With the pasta being precooked it wouldn't be any harder for Charlie to make than it is for him to cook an omelet or hamburger, and I don't know of any restaurants around us that do something like that.

Kelly felt a tap on her shoulder and looked up to see Carola wearing a cover-up top over a bright pink bikini. With her jet black hair and dark skin, she was breathtaking. Her beauty and innate sexiness was not lost on the men in the room, many of whom took the opportunity when their wives or significant others were getting their breakfast to stare longingly at Carola who seemed to be completely oblivious of her charming and sexy appearance.

"I'm going down to the beach and sunbathe this morning. You're welcome to join me," Carola said as she sat down across from Kelly. Sensing something near her feet she looked down. "What do we have here?" she asked, looking at the reclining cat who was purring next to Kelly's feet.

"This is my new friend. He discovered me on the walk here this morning and hasn't left me. I've named him Cayo."

"Here kitty, here kitty," Carola said. Cayo looked at her, but didn't move from his spot next to Kelly. "I thought you told me you were a dog person. I'm the one who has two cats at home. I'd think he'd sense that and come to me."

"Me too. I can't explain this. I know absolutely nothing about cats."

"You might not know anything about them, but I can tell you they are uncanny when it comes to accepting people. If a cat purrs when someone is around, that's a person that can be trusted. If instead a cat hisses, you want to get as far away as you can from that person."

"Thanks, but this might be the only time Cayo and I are together. I imagine he has a lot of friends here. Anyway, thanks for the beach invite, but I need to make sense of the notes I took when we met with the chef yesterday. Why don't we meet here for lunch, say at 1:30? That should give both of us plenty of time. I understand they sell a card which allows you to access the Internet in the lobby. I want to do that and let everyone know we arrived safe and sound. The day we left home there was a hurricane in Mexico that looked pretty bad, and I'm sure my staff and children are wondering if we've been affected by it. See you later."

Kelly stood and started to walk towards the restaurant entrance. As soon as she stood up, Cayo stood up and walked with her step for step. "Kelly," Carola said laughing, "I'll bet you anything you want to bet that this isn't going to be the only time you and Cayo are together. Hope Mike likes cats."

When she got to her room Kelly slid the plastic key card into the slot and the light on the lock turned green. She opened the door and before she could close it, Cayo slipped into the room, jumped on the bed, and curled up on a pillow.

Oh, this is just swell. Our vacation is starting to have a life of its own. Yesterday the death of a fishing guide, and today I've been adopted by a cat. She looked at the calico cat that had fallen sound asleep. *I don't have a clue how Mike is going to feel about this. Dogs we talk about. Cats we've never discussed.*

CHAPTER ELEVEN

Kelly heard the salsa music as soon as she walked down the stairs from their ocean view room and headed for the restaurant. *If the day before yesterday was any indication, I'll bet Carola will be dancing, and every man in the restaurant will be salivating.* As it turned out, it was just as she had predicted. Carola was dancing with a Cuban man to the cheers and hoots of the crowd. Everyone seemed to be having a wonderful time. When Carola saw Kelly she danced over to the table where she'd taken a seat and said, "Be with you in a minute." She and the Cuban man finished the dance to a thunderous round of applause.

"You're really good," Kelly said as Carola sat down. She waved the server over and in fluent Spanish asked for a piña colada. She turned to Kelly. "What can I order for you?"

"I don't know, surprise me. I have no experience with rum drinks."

A few minutes later the server brought them piña coladas. They talked about their families, their husbands, and this and that. Kelly had just looked away from Carola when much to her surprise, she saw Mike walking into the restaurant. She said in a loud voice, "Mike, over here." He walked over to their table and sat down.

"What are you doing here?" Kelly asked. "I thought you were going to be fishing all day and eat lunch on one of the islets like you did yesterday."

"So did I, but the constable sent a boat out for me. The coroner brought his equipment to Cayo Largo earlier today, and he's determined that Dudley was murdered. Apparently it's the first murder that's ever occurred here on the island. The constable wants me to help him, since he's never had to conduct a murder investigation. Plus, Dudley was staying here at the hotel, and we were with him in Havana as well. The constable is picking me up in a few minutes." Mike heard something under the table and looked down. He saw Cayo with his head resting on Kelly's feet.

"What in the devil is this? Never mind, that was a stupid question. I know what it is, but how and why?"

"I have no clue. I was simply adopted by him on my way to breakfast this morning. I think he plans on staying with us while we're here."

"Great. I love our dogs," Mike said, "but I have to tell you it's been kind of nice not having to get up to let them out, make sure they're fed, and all the rest of the stuff that goes along with being a dog owner. What is it with you, Kelly? Do you send out sounds at some tone decibel I can't hear inviting stray dogs and cats to come to you?"

Kelly laughed. "I have no idea. I know nothing about cats, but Cayo seems to have decided we're going to be friends while I'm here."

"Mike, I know you have to go, but does this mean Jack will be a suspect? Where is he?" Carola asked.

"I think everyone who has had anything to do with Dudley will be a suspect. As for Jack, he's still out fishing. There was no need for him to come in with me. I told him to keep fishing and see if he could become a member of the Grand Slam Club." He turned to Kelly. "I have no idea when I'll be back, so if you get hungry tonight go ahead and eat without me."

"Okay, but how do you intend to start this investigation, since it sounds like it's falling into your hands?"

"Several things have happened. Guido, the head fishing guide at the marina, told me when he came to get me in the boat that Philip had volunteered this morning to take over Dudley's group and help them. Guido said he wasn't too sure how he felt about it, because Philip told the group now that Dudley was dead he was going to be the one who would get the exclusive rights from Bartolo to fish in the Cayo Largo area, so they better get to know him."

"What a horrible man," Carola said. "He's saying Jack doesn't have a chance at becoming the exclusive United States agent for Bartolo, right?"

"That's how I'd interpret it. I agree, it takes a lot of nerve to do something like that when a man has been murdered, but I doubt if his clients know that since they're all still out on the water."

"What else has happened?"

Mike looked at his watch, "I'll make this quick, and then I need to go change. The constable will be here in just a few minutes. He spoke with his superior on the main island, and a decision was made to not allow anyone who could be considered a suspect to leave the island, and that includes Dudley's wife. It's somewhat unusual, but he's also decided not to allow Dudley's body to leave Cuba until the killer is found. Jack, Stewart, and Philip, all of whom are the fishing people who might be considered suspects, are here for several more days anyway, but it's unusual to place a hold on the body of a murder victim and not allow the spouse or the decedent's body to be returned to their home country for some type of a memorial service." With that he stood up to leave.

"Wait, Mike, one more thing. What made the coroner say Dudley was murdered rather than suffering a heart attack, which is what was originally thought?" Carola asked.

"He found a little dot on Dudley's arm that looked like a needle puncture. When he conducted the autopsy, he found traces of an unknown substance in Dudley's body. He didn't know exactly which one it was, but it seems to have caused Dudley's heart to stop. Essentially he was poisoned. A lot of coroners would have missed it. I'm pretty impressed the coroner was able to get that information from an autopsy done under rather primitive circumstances. See you later."

Carola, who was normally carefree and vivacious, had become very quiet. After a few minutes she looked at Kelly and said, "I remember you told me how you have helped Mike solve several murder cases in the past. I'm so worried for Jack. Please, Kelly, would you help Mike find the murderer? I'll do what I can to help. Surely my ability to speak Spanish can be of some use. Please, please say yes." She looked at Kelly, her big brown eyes glistening with unshed tears.

"I'll be happy to do anything I can, but we're in a foreign country, at a remote resort, I don't speak the language, and the possible suspects are from all over the world."

"I think the first place to start is with Dudley's widow," Carola said. "She was very rude when I tried to talk to her before, but maybe if I go to her room and offer my condolences, she'll be nicer, and I can find out something."

"From what you told me and what I overheard, I doubt it, but yes, it's worth a try. I wonder where she was when Dudley was murdered. In other words what is her alibi? As to any other suspects, we can forget about Jack, although he was taking a swim, and Dudley was murdered either when he was in the water or right before he was in the water. While Jack might not have a very good alibi, I feel certain we can cross him off the list."

Carola looked steadily at Kelly and said, "I told you before that Jack could not have done it, and that's why I want to find out who did."

"I understand, Carola. That leaves Stewart and Philip. Since they're both out fishing right now, we'll have to wait to find out anything about them. There is someone else that hasn't been mentioned, and this is where your fluency in Spanish might help. I don't think I've told this to you or Mike, but when the guides were showing the men how to cast during the orientation, I went up to the marina building where the fishing equipment is stored to use the bathroom.

"I overheard the head guide, Guido, telling another guide he wanted Jack to be the one to get the contract from Bartolo. I thought it was interesting that he was speaking to his guide in English since he's Italian, and his guide is Cuban. He told the guide he was talking to him in English because he wanted him to use his English as much as he could. He said the reason he wanted Jack to get the contract, and not Dudley, is that Dudley had bragged that when he got the contract he would bring his own people in, and Guido was worried about what would happen to the Cuban guides who had worked so hard to get where they were. He said he considered them family."

"Do you think I should talk to Guido or the one who is guiding Jack?"

"I don't know," Kelly answered. "It just seems to me that maybe one of them would be a suspect if his livelihood was threatened. I don't know if they have families to support or for that matter anything at all about them. Maybe we should take a taxi to the marina and kind of sniff around. We could go to the clubhouse, and you could talk to Guido. We could say I was so charmed by the photos in the clubhouse I wanted to show them to you. Then here's something else that can be done."

"What's that?"

"There's a computer room next to the front desk in the lobby. I'll do an Internet search on Stewart and Philip. Mike will probably get in touch with people he knows back in the States and have them do a background check on everyone involved. I have no idea what we're looking for, but at least we have a few places to start."

"Kelly, let's not waste time. I'll go to the marina and talk to Guido while you do the Internet search. That way we can get a lot more done. When I come back I'll go to Dudley's wife's room and give her my condolences. Why don't we meet in the lobby at 4:00 and share what, if anything, we've learned?"

"Sounds good. I need to go to my room and get some money for the Internet. It will probably take me more time to do the searches than I have left on my existing card. See you at 4:00." Kelly left the table, Cayo at her side. It was obvious Cayo was well-known at the hotel, since no one associated with the resort even bothered to look at him.

CHAPTER TWELVE

Carola paid the taxi driver after he'd driven her the short distance to the marina. She saw several shops that catered to fisherman, went into one of them, and asked where the Bartolo fishing clubhouse was located. The clerk pointed to a building near the dock. As she walked the short distance to it she admired the well maintained dock and large patio with its teak tables and chairs that overlooked the marina. To the left of the patio was a glass windowed office next to a wooden door with several kinds of fish painted on it along with the words "Grand Slam Club."

So that's what Mike was talking about when he mentioned Dudley had caught the tarpon, permit, and bonefish that allowed him to become the first English member of the Grand Slam Club, Carola thought. *Wonder if that provided the motive for someone who wanted to kill him.*

She decided to go in and introduce herself to the handsome Italian man sitting at the desk. Although Carola's beauty was not all that important to her, she was well aware of the effect she had on men and decided that if ever there was a time to make use of it, this was the time.

"Hello. I'm Carola. My husband, Jack, is fishing with one of your guides today. He told me how beautiful the clubhouse and grounds were, and I decided to come and see for myself. I'm also interested in looking at all of the photos on the wall. I hope you don't mind," she said, smiling and batting her long dark eyelashes at him. The poor man never had a chance. He was practically stuttering as he said, "I am Guido Naraldi. I am in charge of the fishing guides. Please have a seat. May I get you something to drink? I would be happy to show you around if you would like to take a tour."

"Thank you, but I just had lunch. I can see that you're busy, so I won't trouble you for a tour. Actually, I'm writing an article for a magazine. I'm surprising my husband with it, and since he spoke so highly of Bartolo Fishing Adventures last night, I thought it would be a fun thing to include something about Bartolo in the article. If you could spare a few minutes of your time, I'd love to ask you some questions."

"For you, I can spare all the time you need. Please, tell me how I can help," he said leaning against the edge of his desk.

"Well, for starters, could you tell me about your company, Bartolo Fishing Adventures? How does it work?"

"Sure, I'd be happy to tell you about the company. Bartolo is an international recreational sport fishing company. We specialize in full service destination sport fishing. By that I mean our customers pay a flat fee for their trip, and that covers everything, including airfare, ground transportation, meals, lodging, and of course fishing equipment and guides. The company is headquartered in Italy and manages different fishing locations throughout the world.

"Our operation here in Cuba is somewhat unique. A number of years ago the company negotiated an agreement with the Cuban government that grants the company the exclusive right to fish in the marine sanctuary located adjacent to Cayo Largo. Fishermen from all over the world come here for our world class fly fishing to catch bonefish, permit, and tarpon."

"I asked my husband if it was crowded out on the water yesterday, and he told me no. With so many people wanting to fish here, how do you do that?"

"The area where we fish is a protected government marine sanctuary, and the only type of fishing allowed is catch and release. We not only strictly adhere to the catch and release of the fish, but we also limit the number of fishermen in each area. We divide the fishable areas around this part of the island into five zones, and no more than three boats are allowed in each zone on the same day."

"Since the embargo is still in effect, American fishermen can't fly directly to Cuba, but once it's lifted they will be able to fly to Cuba from the United States. At that time there will be many American fishermen who will want to come here," Guido said. "When it happens we expect there will be a huge increase in our business. That is why Bartolo wants to have a contract with a fishing guide that will be responsible as their exclusive agent in America to recruit fishermen to come here to Cayo Largo to fish."

"Will you still limit the number of boats allowed and adhere to the catch and release tradition?" Carola asked in a sexy voice.

"Absolutely. Without those two things in place this area would quickly be fished out, and then who would want to come?" Guido shrugged and turned the palms of his hands up.

"I agree, but if this area is open to fishing guides from various foreign countries, what will happen to the Cuban fishing guides?"

"Aah, that is something that keeps me awake at night. I have hired the best guides in Cuba for our company. They work for us at a great sacrifice. They are local and know these waters like the backs of their hands. They spend twenty days working for me, and then they get ten days off to be with their families. It is a great sacrifice to them, but the money is good, actually better than they could make anywhere else in Cuba."

"You said they go to see their families on the ten days they have off. Does that mean their families are not here on Cayo Largo with them?"

"Yes, that is correct. It is not an ideal situation, but there are no schools, and there is no housing for families here on the island. There aren't even any dogs, because there are no permanent residents. The guides live four to a room in housing we provide during the fishing season. Almost all of them have built homes for their families on the Island of the Youth which is about three hours from here by boat.

"If I may speak frankly, *Senora,* I would like to see your husband get the contract from Bartolo to become the exclusive representative in the United States to book American fishermen who want to come to Cuba and fish with us. I understand that one of the contenders for that contract, Dudley Samms, died late yesterday. I can't say that I'm sorry. He told me he planned to bring in his own guides when he got the contract, and that he would let my men go."

"That must have been very hard for you to accept. It sounds like you really care for your employees."

"I do, *Senora,* they are like sons to me, sons I never had. Maybe the God we believe in helped us by allowing *Senor* Samms to die. I heard he had a heart attack while he was swimming. I understand the coroner is going to be flown in from the main island to conduct an autopsy. When the constable told me to take my boat out and bring *Senor* Reynolds back here to the clubhouse, I thought maybe he had learned something. Have you heard anything more about the cause of *Senor* Samms' death?"

"Yes. He was murdered. The legal authorities have begun investigating the murder. I assume you have a good alibi for the time he was murdered. I believe he was murdered after he became qualified to become a member of the Grand Slam Club. It looks like his death was somewhere between 5:30 and 6:30 p.m. last night. I'm sure the authorities will want to know where you were during that time. Do you know if Dudley planned on having you stay on as the chief guide?"

Guido's eyes narrowed as he looked at her. *There is far more to this woman than a beautiful face and a sexy body. It's almost as if she's grilling me on behalf of the authorities. My instincts tell me I better be very, very careful what I say to her.*

"*Senor* Samms told me he planned to keep me on, because I knew the business side of guiding. He said he was an expert at fishing and getting people to pay to come on trips with him. He told me if he was the one chosen by the company to receive the contract allowing him to fish the waters of Cayo Largo, I was going to stay in my current position. As far as last night between 5:30 and 6:30, I have to admit I was with a friend of mine, a woman I meet with from time to time, if you know what I mean," he said grinning. "After all, the fishermen had all returned for the night, and I was officially off work. It's a lady whose company I enjoy, and from what she tells me, she enjoys my company as well," he said with a proud look on his face.

"Of course, and I can certainly see why she would enjoy your company," Carola said, smiling beguilingly up at him. "You've been more than gracious to me. Thank you. From what Jack tells me, you are very good at what you do. I feel like I am so much better informed. Oh, one other thing. I heard that a man named Philip volunteered to act as the guide for the group that Dudley had brought with him."

"That's true. He rode in the van with them this morning and told me they had agreed he would act as their fishing guide while they were here now that their guide was deceased. I don't quite understand what that's all about. Philip has fished with one of our guides for only two days and now he feels that he's qualified to be the head guide for those people? I find it very strange. I have heard he also very much wants to get the Bartolo contract to bring people in from the United States, just as your husband wants to do."

"*Senor*, I agree. I met him, and he seemed very strange to me. I must go now, but I thank you again for your time."

"It has been my pleasure," the handsome Italian man said as he leaned forward trying to sneak a peek down the front of Carola's low-cut blouse. "If I may be of further service, and I mean any kind of service, please feel free to call on me."

"I'll remember that. Thank you."

He's very handsome, and he's very smooth. I wouldn't be at all surprised if he knows a lot more than what he's telling me. He was passionate about his men and if their jobs are in danger, for some men of principle, that could be reason enough to commit murder. I hate to think it, but it seems he could qualify as a suspect.

CHAPTER THIRTEEN

Kelly walked into the small Internet office at the hotel and purchased an Internet access card from the woman behind the desk who was wearing the standard uniform of the hotel, a white blouse and a black skirt. The only difference between the uniform of the male employees and the female employees was that the male employees wore black pants. The one thing Kelly didn't understand is why the women were required to wear hose when the humidity was so high that as soon as you left an air conditioned room your clothing and your body were instantly wet from perspiration.

Following the instructions the young woman gave her she accessed the Internet. She decided to start with a Facebook search for Philip Montgomery because Carola clearly didn't like him, and Kelly was only one step behind her. She hoped he'd put his photograph on Facebook, so she could make sure she had the right person before she got very far into her search. She felt it was very strange that he wanted to become a fishing guide, and yet he'd come to Cuba by himself and was fishing alone each day, at least before he took over Dudley's group.

When she typed in the name Philip Montgomery she discovered she had the right name. The photograph on the Facebook page was clearly the same as the man she'd been with in Havana and who was now here at the resort. She quickly read what he'd written on his timeline, the last entry being the day before she'd met him in Havana.

It was about how he was going fishing in Cuba and probably wouldn't be able to post for a couple of weeks. Under relationship status he had written that he was separated from Miriam Montgomery. He said he missed his son, but when he and his wife had come back to the United States from Australia they realized they really had nothing in common, and they mutually agreed to file for divorce.

Kelly jotted down the name of his wife, intent on finding out what she could about her when she finished researching Philip. She continued to read Philip's page. He'd written that he'd loved to fish all his life, and now that he and his wife were going to get divorced, there was nothing to hold him back from realizing his dream. Cuba seemed like the perfect place for him to make his dream come true, particularly since the embargo on Cuba would probably soon be lifted.

He'd written that he hoped to become the exclusive representative for fly fishermen from the United States who wanted to fish in Cuba, and that was the purpose of his trip to Cuba. He said he knew there were several other people who also had the same idea, but since he'd always gotten whatever he wanted, he had no doubt he would be successful and obtain the exclusive rights to guide American fly fisherman on the island of Cayo Largo in Cuba. Kelly thought it was rather ominous that he went on to write he planned on doing whatever was necessary to insure he would be the one selected to receive the exclusive contract with Bartolo. There were a number of photographs of him with game fish he had caught from different places all around the world. He listed his present residence as the Florida Keys.

After Kelly read everything she could find on his Facebook page, she pulled up the twitter name he had on his Facebook timeline. @PhilipDMontgomery had 20,235 friends on twitter. Kelly wondered how many of them were associated with fishing, and if that's where he intended to get some of his future clientele from.

She returned to Facebook and entered the name of Miriam Montgomery. Nothing came up. Next she put Miriam's name into the google search engine and discovered that Philip's soon-to-be-ex-wife was from an extremely wealthy family who lived in Connecticut. Evidently she'd married Philip and moved to Australia with him, so Philip could work in the family business owned by his parents, the boutique hotel industry. They had a young son, and she had recently separated from Philip and moved to Connecticut to be with her family.

Although she had a law degree from Yale, she had never practiced law. Recently she'd told a reporter who had asked her if she intended to work when she was divorced that she'd already been hired by a top law firm in the area. She'd gone on to say when the final arrangements were made she would make a statement to that effect. Kelly thought it was interesting something like that would show up on a google search. It certainly reiterated that the family was not only very wealthy, but also newsworthy. She wondered if it was Miriam's money that allowed Philip to travel throughout the world while seemingly being unemployed.

He doesn't look like someone who would be into selling drugs, although I've read there are a number of places in the Florida Keys where that type of activity is fairly common. Better check some more on him. She entered his name into the google search engine and discovered that he, too, came from a wealthy family who had lived in Connecticut before they had bought several boutique hotels in Australia. They catered to groups that were interested in fishing in the rivers and the waters surrounding Australia. Philip's Fishing Excursions was listed prominently on all of the family hotel sites. Evidently he had run that part of the business when he was there. There was a note that he had left the family business to open up a fishing guide business in the United States.

Kelly couldn't put her finger on it, but something bothered her about the whole thing. If a marriage was breaking up, why would someone leave his family and return to the United States, settle where he probably didn't know anyone, and attempt to start a new business, a business which had some stiff competition from well-known guides in the form of Jack from the United States and Dudley from England.

She continued to read and after about twenty minutes, found a reference to a twenty-three year old newspaper article. She clicked on the link and read it. She sat back in her chair and tried to take in the enormity of what she'd just read. It was an article with the headline "Wealthy College Student Accused of Murder." The article went on to say Philip Montgomery had been arrested for the murder of Patrick Murphy, a college student from Ireland. The article stated that Patrick had died after an altercation with Philip during a poker game. Several of the college students who had been playing poker had left to go to a nearby bar. From what the article said, one of the students heard Patrick accuse Philip of cheating. He hadn't thought much about it and had joined the others at the bar.

An hour later Patrick's body was found and based on what the college student told the police, Philip was arrested for murder. His bail was quickly posted by his wealthy parents. That was the end of the newspaper article. Kelly continued searching for more information, fruitlessly. She'd jotted down the name of the newspaper and the date of the article, and entered those in the google search engine. She found a second article about the arrest of Philip Montgomery. The article said the case had been dropped due to lack of evidence. There was simply no firm evidence to link the murder of Patrick Murphy to Philip Montgomery. The article ended with a reference to the fact that Philip Montgomery had been expelled from Dartmouth for cheating. Although nothing overt had been written, Kelly felt that was a snide implication that if someone was expelled from a top university for cheating, they could also be capable of murder.

The blinking light on the clock on the bottom right of the computer screen indicated that her time on the computer had expired. She stood up and stretched, wondering how Carola's meeting with Guido had gone. She walked out of the computer room and almost bumped into Carola, who had just gotten out of a taxi. "Kelly, I need to talk to you. See that couch over there?" she said, pointing at one of the many couches scattered around the large open-air lobby. "Let me pay the driver, and I'll meet you there in two minutes."

They spent the next hour sharing with each other what they'd found out. "Carola, I think what Guido told you is certainly of interest, but while you were at the marina talking to him I was thinking that one of the actual fishing guides would have more of a motive to kill Dudley than Guido. After all, from what Guido said, his job was not going to be jeopardized if Dudley got the Bartolo contract, but his guides' jobs might be. I wonder how many guides work for him. It seems a far stretch, but I suppose any of them could be desperate enough about his job that he might kill Dudley."

"Guido had to take a phone call while I was there and when he was on the phone I walked around the room. There were photographs of ten guides. I suppose any of them would have reason to do it, or let me really go far out here, maybe it was a joint effort by more than one of them."

"Wow! I hadn't thought of anything like that. Maybe they all wanted Dudley dead and they drew straws or something like that to decide who would do it. If that's true, I don't have a clue how we could get that kind of information from them."

"Something just occurred to me," Carola said. "If Mike is going to be helping the constable, he's not going to be able to fish until this is solved. Maybe I could take his place on the boat and start a conversation with the fishing guide. He's Cuban, so he obviously speaks Spanish. Jack's Spanish is pretty elementary, and if I spoke fast and so did the guide, I don't think Jack would be able to follow along. I could tell them I just wanted to see what fishing in the saltwater flats was like, and I only wanted to fish for half a day. Actually, I think that would be fine with Jack. He'll have the afternoon to fish exclusively with the guide, and since he's always worried he's abandoning me on these trips, it would make him feel better if he did something for me. I never want to take any of his time away from paying clients, but I think this would work well."

"I agree. It's an excellent way to find out more about the guides. Maybe you'll get the name of one of the guides who feels particularly angry about the possibility of losing his job. Yes, let's see what you can find out tomorrow morning when you go fishing," Kelly said.

"I also need to see if I can get the room number for Dudley's wife, and then I'll pay her a visit. I'll give you a call after I talk to her. What's your room number?"

"We're in 3822, but give me about an hour. I still have a couple of other people I want to check out on the Internet."

"Will do. Good luck and wish me good luck as well," Carola said.

Cayo had followed Kelly from the Internet room and had jumped up on her lap when she sat down. She scratched the cute calico cat behind the ears, and it purred with a sound of deep satisfaction. Kelly stroked Cayo several more times and then stood up, putting him down on the floor. He walked next to her as they returned to the computer room.

CHAPTER FOURTEEN

"I'm hoping you can help me," Carola said in Spanish to the handsome young man at the reception desk. She smiled and opened her eyes wide, so he could clearly see her long lashes and dark brown eyes, while at the same time leaning towards him, and giving him a clear view of her ample cleavage. "I understand that Dudley Samms was killed last night. My husband is a fellow fishing guide, and since I've met his wife numerous times, I would like to visit her and give her my condolences. Would you be kind enough to give me her room number? She gave it to me earlier, but I can't seem to find it."

"We're not supposed to give out room numbers, but in this case I could probably make an exception." He turned his attention away from Carola's chest and looked at his computer. "She's in room 2943. It's a ground floor unit with an ocean view."

"Thank you so much," she said smiling broadly. "I really appreciate your sharing that with me."

"*De nada*, it is nothing," the clerk said, trying unsuccessfully to keep his eyes from straying once again to her chest. She left the reception area and walked towards the rooms located in an outlying building. She paused for a moment and looked at the site map the bellman had given her when they arrived. Patricia's room was the last room in the last unit. When she approached room 2943 she thought she heard voices and looked around. She was the only one in sight.

She distinctly heard a man speaking, and the voice seemed to be coming from the room the clerk had told her was Patricia Samms'. "Patricia, Dudley's dead, and it's about time. Surely you must know how I've felt about you for many years, and although you've never said anything, I think you feel the same way about me. The only reason I ever went on any of Dudley's fishing trips was to be near you. Why else would I put up with him belittling me every chance he got? I fished this morning, but I came back early to see you. Finally, it's our time."

Carola walked to the side of the unit. Since it was the last one on the hotel grounds, there was nothing but brush and the Caribbean Sea beyond it. When she'd walked past the room, she'd noticed the door to Patricia's room was slightly ajar. She flattened herself against the outside wall, listening intently.

"Stewart, I've dreamed of this moment for a long, long time. Since I was married to Dudley, I could never tell you how I felt about you, but yes, I agree, it's our time. Thank you for waiting for me. I suppose it was too bad he had to die, but I feel like I've finally been set free. I hated that man every day of my life, from the day I married him until yesterday, when he finally got what was coming to him."

"I'm just as happy about his death as you are, my dear. It's too soon to celebrate the way I've dreamed of, but come here. Kissing you is something I've wanted to do for so many years, and now I finally can. I have no regrets about what happed to Dudley. He deserved to die."

It was very quiet for a long time and Carola assumed that Stewart was kissing Patricia. *Kelly won't believe this. Stewart and Patricia are an item, and both of them now have good reasons for wanting to see Dudley dead. I wonder if either of them could be the killer. It's too early to call Kelly on her cell phone, but I think I'll go back to my room and make a few notes, so I can tell her exactly what I heard them say.*

*****

"What do you think, Cayo? Who should be next?" Kelly asked the cat after purchasing another one hour Internet access card. Cayo turned his head and looked up at her. She had an uncanny feeling the cat was reading her mind and could swear when he purred it sounded like he'd said the word "Stewart." "Okay, Cayo. Stewart it is."

She typed in the username and the password printed on the Internet access card and began searching for Stewart Bond. Mike had mentioned his name when he was telling her about the van ride and how Dudley had humiliated him. Since Facebook had been such a bonanza for providing information to her about Philip, she decided to start there. The photograph on Stewart Bond's page clearly showed that the man she had seen with Dudley at the rooftop restaurant in Havana was the same man whose picture she was looking at on his Facebook page.

In the information Stewart had provided on his page it said that he was the head of the private wealth division for a large international bank, an avid outdoorsman, and a bachelor. There were a number of photos of him with big game in Africa, a huge king salmon from British Columbia, and bonefish from Belize. He'd graduated with honors from Eton and had gone to law school at Harvard in the United States. When he returned to London he began working for the bank he was still with. He didn't have very many friends on Facebook, just a few hundred, which made Kelly think this was more of a personal page than a business page.

There had been no mention of a twitter account, but even so, she tried putting in several different ways he might have used to enter his name, but she couldn't come up with a match. She typed his name into the google search engine and spent the next half hour reading about him. Almost everything was related to his business or his being an outdoorsman. Evidently he raised Brittany hunting dogs and maintained a large kennel for them several miles outside of London. One of the articles said that his hunting dogs were considered to be some of the best in the world, consistently taking top honors in field trials.

Although there was no lack of information about his vocation and avocation, there was very little information of a personal nature.

Kelly found one reference to him having attended the Queen's Ball with Lady Jane Simpson and another one regarding him attending a polo match with Dame Susan Lester. That was it, and both of those references were over ten years old. It seemed that Stewart Bond was either very discreet or had no personal life. Kelly looked at his Facebook picture again, refreshing her memory of him.

I remember thinking he was attractive when I saw him in Havana. He reminded me a bit of Mike, big and burly. He was greying at the temples and was quite tan, probably from all of this outdoor hunting and fishing which seems to be his passion. Looking at his picture again, I still think he's very attractive, and I find it very hard to believe he wouldn't have romantic interests. Wish I knew how I could find out about that. While Facebook is very good about letting people know what the individual being looked up wants people to know, it sure doesn't help with information they may not want to share. I'm sure Mike will have someone look into his background. Maybe he can get the type of information I can't seem to get.

Kelly's attention was drawn to the clock on the bottom of the screen that had begun to flash indicating she had only a few more minutes left before her allotted time expired. She logged off, looked at Cayo and said, "Okay, little guy. Time to go to the room and wait for Carola's call, but I don't feel this last hour was very productive. Let's go." She moved her chair away from the computer, and she and Cayo walked out of the computer room and headed for her room.

CHAPTER FIFTEEN

Kelly started to put her key card into the lock when she noticed that the door wasn't completely shut, and the lock hadn't engaged. She felt her heart race as she called out, "Hello? Is anyone there? Mike, are you there?" No one answered. She stood to the side and pushed the door open with her foot. Cayo walked into the room and looked back at her as if to say, "Come on, scaredy cat. There's no one here but you and me. All's safe."

She followed Cayo into the room and looked in the bathroom and in the main room. No one was there. *Maybe there's a problem with the locks not fully engaging. I've noticed a few other doors that seemed to be slightly ajar. That would explain it. I think I'm getting spooked with everything that's happened. Calm down, Kelly,* she told herself. *I've done this before. I can help Mike find out who murdered Dudley even though he probably wouldn't approve of what I've been doing this afternoon. Oh well, what he doesn't know won't hurt him.*

She'd just closed and locked the door when the phone in the room rang. "Hi, Carola. What did you find out?" She listened for a few minutes and then said, "Well, that probably explains why I couldn't find out anything about Stewart's personal life. He's been waiting for Patricia all these years, and from what you just told me, it sounds like she's been waiting for him as well. That really makes my crime solving antenna start to wiggle."

"You're right, Kelly, and while I'm new to this detective game which you're so good at, it sure seems to me like either one of them or even both of them could be considered suspects. Killing someone because of a romantic interest is the stuff that books, movies, and television are made of. You know a lot more about this than I do. What do you think?"

"I have no idea. I'll google Patricia tomorrow and see if I can find out anything about her. What's on your schedule now?"

"I've got to go, Kelly. Jack just walked in with a big smile on his face. Must have been good fishing this afternoon. Why don't we meet you in the restaurant at 7:00 for dinner? Maybe Mike will be back by then, and he can join us, but if not, we'll see you then."

Kelly hung up the phone and went into the bathroom, intending to take a cool shower. It didn't take long in this heat and humidity to become wringing wet. She'd just turned the shower on when the phone rang. She turned the shower off and walked back into the bedroom.

"Hello." She listened to the voice on the other end. "Hi, Mike, how was your afternoon?"

"Long. The constable is a very nice man, but he doesn't know a thing about investigating a case like this. I've been on the computer most of the afternoon as well as on the phone with my deputies back home and some other law enforcement personnel I know trying to get information about the people I consider to be suspects. It's been rough slogging because this computer is very slow, but I guess that's the trade-off for being in a beautiful, remote area. The only thing I learned with any certainty is that Philip was once accused of murder, but the case was dropped. He's recently separated from his wife, and no one is quite sure where he's getting the money to live the lifestyle he leads.

"I had his new home in the Florida Keys checked out, and it looks like the guy is made of money. The thing is beautiful. It's right on the water, and according to the county records, he paid three and a half million for it. Not bad for a guy who's unemployed and hoping to make a name for himself as a fishing guide. Doesn't quite add up in my book. We're trying to find the source of where he's getting his money. Anyway, I'm going to spend a couple more hours here, so go ahead and eat dinner without me."

"Carola just called and asked me to dinner. I'll join them. Anything pro or con about Jack?"

"No. I let the constable search Jack's background, because I'm too close to him to be non-judgmental. Fortunately, in the preliminary check the constable thought he had one of the cleanest records he'd ever seen. The only black mark against him is he went for a swim in the ocean at or about the same time that Dudley did, and Dudley later turned up dead. That's a coincidence, and you know what I think about coincidences, but in this case I think it's a legitimate coincidence."

"I do know what you think about coincidences, but sometimes they are simply that, coincidences, and this may be one of those times. I'm off to take a shower. I hope it's air-conditioned where you are, because this heat and humidity is brutal. I'm thoroughly enjoying this island and being here, but I wouldn't want to live in the Caribbean because of the weather."

"Don't think that's anything you need to worry about. The only way we'll be leaving our home in Cedar Bay is feet first. See you later."

Showered and cooled, Kelly locked the door, double-checked it to make sure it had closed securely and walked down the curving path to the restaurant, Cayo walking beside her. She paused for a moment on her way, looking at the aqua blue color of the Caribbean and the flames of pink and blue in the sky as day turned to night. Although it seemed to be the epitome of a place for romance, like so many things, scratch the surface and the ugly appears. In this case the ugly came in the form of murder.

CHAPTER SIXTEEN

When Kelly walked into the restaurant, she immediately saw Carola waving at her. She and Jack were sitting at one of the tables that had a direct line of view from the open front reception area to the ocean. She sat down and said, "So, Jack, how was your second day on the water? What zone were you in today?"

"Zone three, and it was amazing. It's going to be hard to fish anywhere else after fishing here at Cayo Largo. I lost track of the number of fish I caught. Here are a couple of pictures my guide took of me and the fish." He showed her several picture of him holding various different fish.

"Good for you. I'm sure Mike's going to be envious when he sees these. Too bad he can't do what he thought he'd be doing when he came here, but solving a murder usually takes precedence in his world."

"Speaking of Mike," Jack said, "have you heard from him today?"

"Yes, he called a few minutes ago and told me he would be spending a couple more hours with the constable. He said for me to go ahead and join you for dinner, and he'd get something later."

"Have they discovered anything yet? I had no idea what was going on when Guido came out in the boat and got him. Carola told me that the coroner determined that Dudley's death was not accidental."

"She knows as much as I do. I imagine Mike might be able to tell us a bit more when he gets here, but I have no idea when that might be. He did tell me that Philip, the guy from the Florida Keys, just bought a home for three and a half million, and since he's between careers or jobs, no one can figure out where he's getting that kind of money. He also recently separated from his wife who now lives in Connecticut. Prior to moving to Florida he worked for his parents' family business as the manager of several boutique hotels in Australia that his parents own. Mike's having his people try and find out some additional financial information about him."

"Did Mike say anything about me? Am I still considered a suspect?" Jack asked with a tone of concern in his voice.

"I don't know. I think everyone who might have had any type of connection to Dudley will be considered a suspect, so I assume that would include you. Mike did say he told the constable he wanted him to do the background search on you, because he didn't want there to be any hint of a conflict of interest when it came to you because of your relationship with Mike."

"I can appreciate that, but I guarantee you that they won't find anything. I've probably led about as clean a life as anyone can. I've never even gotten a traffic ticket."

"Wish I could say that," Carola said, laughing, I've gotten three or four traffic tickets, and the only thing that's kept me from getting a couple more is smiling at the policeman and batting my eyelashes. For some reason they're suckers for big brown eyes, dark skin, and women who bat their eyelashes at them."

"Don't test your luck, honey. Try that too many times, and you're bound to find the cop who wants it known that he was able to resist the attractions that did in so many of his cohorts. Here's to you and no more speeding tickets." Jack said as he smiled at her and raised his glass. "Don't know about you, but I'm starving. Let's eat."

Cayo seemed to understand every word that was being said and made the rounds of all the tables of the other guests while the three of them were filling their plates. Kelly watched the little cat go from table to table, pausing for a moment, and if it was apparent that the people either hadn't noticed the cat or chose not to give him a scrap of food, he simply went on to the next table until he'd worked the entire room. When he was finished, he returned to the table where Kelly was seated and stretched out under the table next to her legs. In a moment he was sound asleep.

"Jack, I've been thinking," Carola said. "Since it looks like Mike won't be able to go fishing with you tomorrow, and the boat can accommodate one more person, I'd like to go out in the morning with you. I think it would help me when I deal with clients if I could describe the fishing experience with firsthand knowledge. I'll come in at noon, and you can go back out."

"I'd love it Carola, but I'll go you one better. The guide told me he would be taking me to lunch tomorrow at a little restaurant at Sirena Beach. He said they have dolphins there that are trained and some of the best lobster in the world. It's a thatched roof place with nothing around it but the Caribbean and white sand." He turned to Kelly. "Why don't you take a taxi and join us, and then you and Carola could ride back together to the hotel."

"You don't have to ask me twice," Kelly said. "Any time the word lobster is mentioned I'm right there. Thanks. That's something I'll really look forward to. What time should I meet you?"

"The guide told me we'll get off the water at 12:30. We'll meet you then."

"Jack, Mike told me there are very strict fishing regulations here in Cuba. Is that going to be a problem for Carola?"

"Would be if I hadn't gotten a fishing license for her. I always get one for her whenever we go anywhere just in case there's a chance for her to do what she'll be doing tomorrow - experiencing the fishing firsthand. It really does help her sell fishing trips to my clients."

"Sounds great. I think Cayo and I will leave you, so you can have a somewhat romantic evening together. Even though it's humid, it really is beautiful here. I'd suggest a romantic walk on the beach, but given what happened last night, that might not be advisable. See you at 12:30 tomorrow at Sirena Beach. Let's go, Cayo."

CHAPTER SEVENTEEN

"Who is it?" Kelly asked as someone knocked on the door two hours after she and Cayo had returned to the room.

"It's me, sweetheart," Mike said. "Open up." She opened the door and was immediately engulfed in a bear hug.

"What's this all about?"

"Whenever I'm involved in something like this, I'm just so glad you're okay," he said.

"So," she said, looking up at him, "do you know who did it?"

"At the moment I don't have a clue. There are a number of people who might have had a reason to do it, but no one has jumped to the front of the line."

"Mike, you've got to be starving. Go down to the restaurant and get something to eat, and then we can talk."

"Actually, the constable's wife brought dinner to us. It was fabulous. She called it *pollo con arrozo*. He told me it means chicken with rice. Moist, a little sweet, a little tang, and so tender the meat fell off the bone. I could eat that every day, but at the moment I'm stuffed. She also brought us dessert which was a dish she called *tres leches.* It's a cake made with three different kinds of milk, evaporated, condensed, and cream. After I tasted it I wished I'd asked her for the recipe before she left. I know you'd love it."

"Actually, I had it yesterday at the restaurant, and it was delicious. In fact, it was so delicious I asked the chef for the recipe. Thanks for thinking of me. You know I'm always looking for new recipes for the coffee shop, although Cuban food in the sleepy little town of Cedar Bay does seem like a bit of a stretch, but then again, maybe the residents need a food stretch. After talking to the chef, I'm going to try a couple of the recipes and see what happens. "

"Kelly, I'd love to sit here and talk to you all night, but I'm whipped. What are your plans for tomorrow? You'd talked about getting a massage. Any luck with that?"

"I was going to look into it, but Jack made me an offer I couldn't resist. Since you can't go out in the boat tomorrow, Carola's going to take your place, and I'm going to meet them for lunch at some little grass shack restaurant on Sirena Beach. He said the guide told him they have the best lobster in the world that barely cost anything."

"Okay, I'm sold. I'll tell the constable that this is my vacation, and while I don't mind not fishing, I do mind not being able to eat lobster. What time are you meeting them?"

"We're going to meet at 12:30. I'd love it if you could join us."

"Consider it done. Don't get up with me in the morning. I'll go down and have some breakfast before the constable picks me up at 8:00. Enjoy yourself and sleep in. Nite."

"Nite, love."

"Wait a minute, Kelly, what did I just hear? It sounded like a cat purring."

"It was. Cayo's asleep under the bed."

"I would like to ask you how in the devil it is that you find an animal to adopt wherever we go. Remember Caesar, that huge Courser dog that befriended you when we went to that cooking school in Italy? And now we have a cat in Cuba? Never mind. Don't answer. You'd just come up with something that sounded perfectly reasonable to you but not to anyone else. Sleep well my love."

Within moments Mike was peacefully snoring as was Cayo in his lair under the bed. Kelly smiled to herself and drifted off into a dreamless sleep.

CHAPTER EIGHTEEN

"Goodby, and good luck catching the bad guys," Kelly said to Mike the next morning as he left for breakfast. "I'm going back to sleep just because I can." It was a rare luxury for someone who had to open up Kelly's Koffee Shop five mornings a week at 6:00 a.m. to get ready for the crowd who was always there when it opened an hour later.

At 9:30, feeling decadent after sleeping so late, she let Cayo out and kept the door slightly open so he could get back in. She was pretty sure she wouldn't be able to hear him with the air conditioner turned up to its maximum strength, a necessity in the Caribbean. A few minutes later he returned, and after making sure the lock on the door had engaged, the two of them walked to the restaurant. Halfway there Cayo stopped and began eating cat food someone had conveniently placed on the path. It seemed obvious that whoever had put it there had been to the resort before and knew there were cats who would appreciate their foresightedness.

The same server who had brought her coffee the morning before said, "*Hola*," with a wide smile on her face. *Better go light on the food if I'm going to have lobster for lunch, and from what Jack's guide said these are some of the biggest and the best lobsters in the world. Don't want to overdo on breakfast and miss that experience.* After some mango juice and a bowl of fruit, she and Cayo walked out to the white sandy beach. Kelly had read about the island and the resort before coming to Cuba, and according to what she'd read, this was one of only two beaches in the world that had this type of fine white sand. Supposedly it didn't stick to you even if you were wet from the ocean or simply sticky from the humidity. After a long walk on the beach and feeling she'd be able to justify the lobster because of it, she turned back to the steps that led to the resort and her room.

I didn't think cats liked water, but evidently no one bothered to tell Cayo. He never left my side during my walk on the beach, even if he did always keep to the side of me that was away from the water. Time to get back to the room, freshen up as best I can, and in this heat that isn't going to be easy, and then off to lunch. Think I'll leave Cayo outside while I'm gone, and he can beg for a little food from the other guests.

A short time later she walked up to the large uniformed security guard standing beside the reception desk and asked him if he would order a cab for her.

"Of course, *Senora*. Where are you going today?"

"Sirena Beach Restaurant. I'm meeting some friends. Is the food good there?"

"I hear it's spectacular, but I've never been there."

"Why not?" Kelly asked.

"There are certain places we Cubans are not allowed to go on the island, and that is one of them. I have gone to the beach, but never the restaurant. The lobster there is supposed to be wonderful, and I hear there is a large enclosed pen which has two dolphins in it that are trained and do tricks for the tourists when they go there for lunch."

"I'm looking forward to it, but I don't understand why Cubans can't go there."

"Those places are reserved for the tourists. You'll notice you never see any Cuban locals here at the resort in the restaurants or the bars. The Cuban guides who take the people fishing are not allowed to be in any of the hotels on the island."

"That doesn't sound fair. Why not?"

"As I said, this island is designated for tourists only. There is nothing here for the Cuban people. Ah, here is your taxi. Enjoy your lunch."

Kelly stepped up into the taxi van along with several other people. There was one paved road on the island, and the road to Sirena Bach was not part of it. The van swerved to the left and the right trying to dodge the numerous potholes, finally coming to a stop at a large open-air restaurant next to a white sand beach. The sunny sky and the color of the Caribbean Sea as it changed from green to aqua, along with the white sand, made Sirena Beach a picture perfect postcard.

The driver opened the door and Kelly, along with the other passengers, departed. She paid the driver, still clueless as to the difference between pesos and the Cuban pesos marked "pesos convertibles." The beach was on her left with palm trees swaying in the gentle breeze. On her right was water, with a fence surrounding it on three sides and a dock making up the fourth side. Beyond that were the saltwater flats.

Wonder if that's where the dolphins are. I have no idea how much water they need to feel like they're in the wild, and why would they be trained at a remote island like Cayo Largo where almost no one would ever see them? This is going to be interesting.

She walked into the large thatched roof open-air restaurant and stood for a moment thinking that she'd stepped onto a movie set. A long wooden bar was on her right and beyond that was the clear shallow water of the Caribbean. On her left was the beach with water that seemed to stretch forever. "*Hola,*" the man behind the bar said, smiling as he greeted her. A handful of people sat at picnic style tables and at the bar. She saw two men walking over to the enclosed pen beyond the bar. One of them got into the water and was immediately greeted by two dolphins. The second man walked out on the dock and stepped down onto a small raised platform. He tossed some fish from a container into the water, and the dolphin show began.

For the next fifteen minutes the dolphins performed numerous acrobatic tricks. They kissed one of the men, flapped their fins, twisted, turned, dove deep, and then shot out of the water doing somersaults. Kelly couldn't help herself from clapping, and she became aware of someone next to her doing the same. "Hey, pretty lady," Mike said, "I just got here, and I'm glad I didn't miss the show. Pretty amazing, isn't it? Back in the States we'd pay dearly to see something like this. Think the cost of admission at Sea World in San Diego is about seventy or eighty dollars per person, and we're getting all of this for free. This is worth the cost of the trip. Never thought we'd see our own private dolphin show when we decided to come down here."

Just then Kelly saw Jack and Carola approaching in one of the fishing boats. *She's holding her thumbs up so they must have caught some fish,* Kelly thought.

She and Mike walked over to the small boat as the guide expertly nudged it onto the shore. He helped Carola out of the boat as Jack easily jumped out of it. "You won't believe what I caught," she said. "Two bonefish and a tarpon. I'm not a fisherperson, but that had to be one of the most exciting mornings I've ever spent in my life. And the views, they were absolutely incredible." She stood and looked around, noticing the people walking away from where the dolphins had been performing. "Looks like we missed the show. How was it?"

"Probably as good as your morning," Kelly answered. "I feel like one of the most fortunate people in the world to have seen it."

Mike walked over to the bar, took the beers he'd ordered, and handed one to Kelly. "When it's as hot as it is here, the only thing that makes any sense to drink is an ice cold beer. These are so cold they must have been in the freezer." He took a sip. "That might just be the best beer I've ever had in my life. Let's sit down and order. I told the constable I was coming here for lunch, but I told him I wouldn't be staying long."

The waiter motioned them over to a table and handed them a menu. At the bottom right was the lobster. Carola leaned over and said, "Our fishing guide said the lobsters are usually two to two and a half pounds. I think we may just be the luckiest people in the world to be here. I mean, how many people know about this place? There are maybe ten to fifteen people here, and we're getting ice cold beer, dolphin shows, and huge lobster tails for almost nothing, and I can't leave out the view. Yup, I'm definitely coming back. Of course, that's assuming Jack isn't arrested for murder," she said laughing.

Mike wasn't smiling. She looked at him very closely. "Mike, is there something you need to tell us?"

"No, not really. Kelly always asks me if I've caught the bad guys yet. We haven't caught the bad guys, but there sure seem to be a few people who might qualify as bad guys. I found out from a contact of mine in England that even though it was never in the press, it was well-known among the upper class British that Stewart Bond's in love with Dudley's wife, and has been for many years."

"Do you think Dudley knew that? Maybe that's the reason he publicly humiliated Stewart," Kelly asked.

"I don't know, and I'm not sure how we could ever find that out unless Dudley kept a diary or something, and nothing I've found out about the man leads me to believe he was the type to do that."

"Anything else?"

"Well, we're taking a long look at Philip Montgomery. One of my sources got back to me this morning after doing a little research on his finances. For the last few years his bank account has received very large monthly deposits from a trust account that's in his wife's name, although he's been authorized by her to write checks on it. Her grandparents set it up for her when she was born, and when she turned thirty-five the bulk of it was given to her outright. For the last six months large transfers have been made to a bank account in the Cayman Islands that stands in the name of Philip Montgomery. Hate to say anything, but looks like Philip is ripping off his wife's account."

"Even if he is, what does that have to do with Dudley's murder?"

"I don't know, but it certainly is coincidental, and Kelly knows how I feel about coincidences. Plus, there's talk that Philip separated from his wife because she has colon cancer. From what I learned, she's under heavy sedation most of the time from the pain. I only found one item about her having cancer, so I can only assume that her press staff, and being that wealthy, I assume she has one, is trying to keep people from knowing about it. Neither one of her parents is in very good health, and she's hired a nanny to take care of their infant son."

"But wouldn't she know if large withdrawals were being taken out of her account?" Carola asked.

"If she were healthy, of course, but when someone is suffering from colon cancer, they're usually in excruciating pain. Couple that with parents in ill health, your husband separating from you, and trying to take care of a toddler. I doubt that keeping an eye on her bank account has been her primary concern. And don't forget if someone has had plenty of money all of their life, they tend to think it will always be there. In this case, while she's not destitute, it looks like she may not be as wealthy as she thinks she is. It also explains how Philip has been able to be unemployed, go on trips like this one, and afford a three and a half million dollar waterfront home in the Florida Keys."

They were all quiet for a few moments. "Mike, what about Dudley's wife, Patricia? Stewart may have loved her for many years, but what if it was returned? What if she and Stewart had been having an affair for a number of years, and Dudley found out about it? What if he threatened to expose them? They were both members of the English elite, and Stewart has a very prestigious and high paying job with an international bank. The bank might not look favorably on having one of their foremost bankers exposed for having an affair with a married woman."

"Kelly," Mike said looking closely at her, "Why do I get the feeling you know things I don't know. I thought we'd decided several cases ago that you were not going to get involved in my cases."

"Mike, I'm not getting involved in anything. I just happened to overhear a couple of women talking while I was getting lunch yesterday. I wasn't snooping or anything. You know I would never do that," she said with her fingers crossed behind her back. "Oh my gosh, here come the lobsters. I've never seen anything like this."

They all turned to look at the two waiters who were walking towards them. Mike turned back to Kelly. "I'll table this for now, but this discussion is not over."

The only sounds heard for the next few minutes were sounds of pleasure as each of them expressed their view that they'd never had a lunch or even a meal, quite like this one. When they were finished, Carola said, "I've eaten all over the world and had more wonderful meals than I can remember, but I think this may be my favorite. It was not only the lobster which was the biggest and the best I've ever had, but the ambiance, the colors of the water, everything. This was simply perfect. I wouldn't change a thing." She stood up, and as she walked over to the table where Jack's guide was sitting she said over her shoulder, "Finish up. I want to talk to Pedro for a few minutes."

Jack looked over at her and smiled fondly. "No matter where we go, she loves to find out about the people and the culture. I can make out a couple of words she's saying to Pedro, and I think that's what she's doing now. I'm a very lucky man to have her as my wife, and never does a day go by that I don't know it."

"Doing what you do, I couldn't agree more." Mike said. "Her ability to speak several languages alone would be important for someone in your business, but she has something else, something you can't bottle. It's a love of people and life. She's very charismatic, and people are drawn to her. That's something that can't be learned. You either have it or you don't." He glanced at his watch. "Kelly I've got to get back. I promised the constable I wouldn't be gone long. Sit here and enjoy this, because we probably won't be passing this way again. See you tonight." He kissed her and stood up. "And by the way, I'll let you pay my share," he said, winking at Kelly. "A taxi just pulled up, and since there are only two on the island, I better grab it while it's here."

CHAPTER NINETEEN

When they got back to the hotel after their lunch at Sirena Beach, Carola said, "Kelly, let's go up to my room, and I'll tell you what I learned from Jack's guide."

"I'd love to hear what he said, but let's go to my room instead. I know it sounds ridiculous, but I have a feeling Cayo is waiting for me to come back. Having never had a cat, I don't know if that's true, but it's just a feeling I have."

A few minutes later they climbed the stairs to Kelly's oceanfront room and there, lying down in front of the door waiting for Kelly's return, was Cayo. Kelly unlocked the door, and Cayo and Carola walked into the room. "Wow, you've got a better view than we do," Carola said. "We're on the second floor and while we're on the ocean side, we don't have a view like this." She turned away from the view and sat down in the rattan chair with its blue upholstered seat and ottoman, both of which matched the main color theme of the room, ocean blue. Hand-painted stars, the moon, and the sun decorated the walls.

"Well, I'm dying of curiosity. What did you find out?" Kelly asked.

"Pedro has been working here for several years. They money is good, and he has been able to build houses for his aging parents and his growing family. I think we discussed how the guides work for twenty days, and then they go home to their families for ten days. He says it's a hard life, but it's allowed him to do a lot for his family. I asked him what would happen to him if a new person became the head guide and brought in their own guides. He said it wouldn't make any difference to him. There are other fishing guide companies on some of the other islands, and he could always get a job with one of them. He said the arrangement with them is about the same as what he's paid by Bartolo. He likes working for Guido and would really miss that, but Pedro said he has a reputation as being one of the best guides on the island, and he's certain he could easily find work."

"Did you ask him about the other guides?"

"Yes. He said almost all of them could easily find employment as fishing guides. Bartolo is considered to be the best fishing guide company on the islands, so other companies would be more than happy to hire any of their guides. He did say there was one guide who was probably going to be leaving at the end of the season."

"Why?"

"Well, this is interesting," Carola said. "Evidently the guides and Guido keep track of how many fish are caught each day, and they post the results of each day's fishing on a bulletin board in the clubhouse. It also indicates the name of each guide and how many fish his clients caught on that day. At the end of the season if it's apparent that the overall catch of a certain guide is much lower than the others, he's fired, and a new one is hired. Pedro said Rico was probably going to be fired at the end of the season. He said it was common knowledge among the guides that even though Rico is married to Guido's cousin, Guido will have to let him go."

"So even if someone else took over as the exclusive representative for Bartolo, Rico would probably be fired?"

"Yes, and he said a change in management would have nothing to do with Rico's abilities as a guide. He said Guido would have to get rid of him to save his own job, because Rico wasn't producing. Not much difference from back in the United States when someone has to sell a certain amount of something, say insurance, and if they don't produce, they're fired, and someone else is hired who promises they can deliver."

"So what you're saying, based on your conversation with Pedro, is that he wouldn't qualify as a suspect, and since we're pretty much ruling out Guido because he has nothing personally to gain or lose by someone else coming in and being Bartolo's exclusive representative, we can stop looking at the guides as suspects. Listen to me talk, I say 'we' as if we have anything to do with this case. As Mike constantly points out to me, it's his case, not mine," she said laughing. "And although I know technically he's right, I still think we can find out a few other things that might help solve the case."

"So what do we do now?" Carola asked.

"I'm going to get on the computer again and see what I can find out about Patricia, Dudley's wife. If she's in love with Stewart, and from everything we've heard she seems to be, I think we need to find out more about her. Do you have any other ideas?"

"This is going to sound weird, but I'm going to go with you to the computer room and see what comes up when I search for Jack. I know he would never kill anyone, but maybe if there is something about him that's negative I would be able to know about it ahead of time and warn him before the constable interviews him. Even though Mike said the constable had pretty much given Jack a clean bill of health when he searched for him on the Internet, I'd feel better if I did it, too. It's probably just a matter of time until the constable wants to interview him again."

"Actually, I think that's a very good idea. So, let's look at who we have left. We've ruled out the Cuban guides, so that leaves Patricia, Stewart, Philip, and I hate to say it, Carola, but I suppose technically Jack is still a suspect."

"Yeah, hard to think of your husband as a murder suspect, but yes, I suppose he is."

"I had to go through that once with Mike when his aunt was murdered in Calico, California. It was one of those things of who has the most to gain when someone is murdered. In this case it was Mike because she willed everything to him, and her estate was quite sizable. I felt sick to my stomach until the murder was solved, and Mike was no longer a suspect.

"To change the subject, I wonder why all of those men are carrying the chaise lounges up from the beach. Do you think we're going to get some weather? I read where it usually rains every day here in the tropics, and I've been thinking how lucky we've been that it hasn't rained. Maybe our luck is about to change for the worse. Perhaps they know something we don't know. When we get back from our computer searches, I'll see if I can find an English language television station that has something on it about the weather."

"Okay, let's go. I want to get this over with. I enjoyed lunch today, but I definitely am not enjoying the prospect of having to do a computer search to see if the constable missed something about my husband, and I find out he could be a viable suspect in a murder case."

CHAPTER TWENTY

Kelly and Carola walked into the computer room and each of them purchased an Internet access card. For the next hour neither one of them spoke. When the flashing clock on the computer screen indicated Kelly had thirty seconds left on her card, she logged off and turned to Carola who had done the same.

"Let's get a piña colada to take to the room and share what we found out. I'll buy," Carola said, grinning.

"Gee, thanks, what an offer considering all the drinks here at the hotel are free. The only money I've seen on the bar or anywhere else is for tips, and as hard-working and gracious as the hotel employees are, they deserve all the tips they can get." As they walked out of the computer room, Cayo stood up and dutifully followed them.

.

"Go ahead and have a piña colada. Maybe being from Chile you're used to this humidity, but for me," Kelly said, "I think an ice cold beer would taste more refreshing than a rum drink."

A few minutes later they were standing in front of the large windows in Kelly's room that looked out at the ocean. On the horizon dark storm clouds hung above the bright clear aqua colored water of the Caribbean Sea. "Carola, when we go down to dinner, would you ask the receptionist if they're expecting some weather? Those dark clouds, coupled with the staff removing the chaise lounges from the beach area, makes me nervous. Okay, you go first."

"I googled Jack's name. It's kind of a funny thing because his father was a teacher, but he was also a fishing guide in the summer. When Jack decided to become a guide he left off his surname, Reynaldo, and used the name Jack Trout. Actually, Trout is his middle name. I'm sure some people wonder about it, but it legitimately is his name. Sorry, I digressed. There were a number of references to him and all the awards he's won as a fishing guide. When I pulled up fly fishing guides for the United States, his name came up first. He's told me several times before that his name is at the top of the list, but I was really impressed when I saw it for the first time with my own eyes. I'd never looked before."

"What about Facebook? Did you try that?"

"No. I go on his Facebook page from time to time, so I'm pretty familiar with it. Kelly, I know Jack's my husband, and I'm biased, but there is absolutely nothing derogatory about him anywhere. He's squeaky clean. He's never been married other than to me, there aren't any children born out of wedlock, and there are no arrest records concerning him, absolutely nothing. The only two strikes he has against him is first, he could benefit from Dudley's death as that would mean one less competitor for the Bartolo contract, and secondly, he happened to go for a swim at the same time Dudley was swimming and then his body was discovered. That's it. I can't imagine that anyone in law enforcement would try and make a case against him based on those two things. Actually, from a layman's perspective, I don't think there is a case to be made."

"I couldn't agree more with you, and I'm sure Mike would agree as well. He's told me several times when I've mentioned possible suspects that if he was teaching Suspect 101, he'd give a student an F if he or she thought a suspect should or could be charged based on evidence as flimsy as what there is against Jack."

"Okay, that takes care of Jack. What did you find out about Dudley's wife, Patricia?"

"She's from a family whose pedigree goes back centuries in England. Seems like everybody in her family was an earl or a duke or a dame. She's from the south of England, and her parents had a huge castle there. She's an only child, so for the first time in the family's history, there was no male heir to pass it on to when her parents died. She inherited the castle and the income from all the lands surrounding it. She and Dudley lived there, and he commuted to London when it was necessary. The area she's from is well-known for its superb fishing. People come from all over the world to fish the rivers there, and Dudley was the boy wonder of the area when it came to fishing expertise."

"Sounds like you googled Dudley as well."

"I did. It didn't take long to find out everything about Patricia. Oh, one thing I didn't mention. Naturally she went to private schools, and she graduated with honors from Cambridge. There was one reference to the fact she wanted to be a doctor, but her parents felt that a marriage to a man who had a pedigree to match hers, and evidently Dudley did, was far more important. They wanted the best for their daughter. Women of her class were not usually women who worked for a living."

"Wow. Kind of explains why it doesn't sound like their marriage was one made in heaven. She wanted to be a doctor, and then her parents tell her she has to marry Dudley. Who knows? Maybe she and Stewart were lovers in college or something. I know this might be a stretch, but if either one of them or both of them was unhappy enough, and the cause of their unhappiness was Dudley, maybe they decided to get rid of him and take a stab at happiness."

"Could be," Kelly said. "Here's what I found out about Dudley. His family goes back in history about as far as hers, but after he and Patricia were married it was discovered his father had a gambling addiction, and he lost the family castle and all the land surrounding it on one bet in a poker game. His mother died soon afterwards. The article I read said she died from shame. His father followed her in death in less than six months. The article indicated that while it was never proven, the evidence pointed to the fact he had taken his own life."

"So Patricia was more or less forced to marry Dudley because of his impeccable lineage, and then her father-in-law loses everything on the turn of a card," Carola said. "Her mother-in-law dies, and her father-in-law commits suicide. It's no wonder Dudley and Patricia never got divorced. He may have wanted to get rid of her, but she was his ticket to still being a member in good standing of the elite class of English society. If his father lost everything, there's a good chance he was living off of her money as his was gone. There was no way he would ever let her go."

"That's true," Kelly said. "And it certainly seems to me that Patricia would have a very good reason to want him dead. Not only would she be free to pursue her relationship with Stewart, she'd be rid of a leech that was living off her money. I don't have any idea what fishing guides make, but I don't think it's on par with someone who owns a huge castle in England and receives income from all the surrounding lands."

"You've got that right. It's almost time for Jack to come back. Think I'll go down and see if the front desk has any information on a possible storm, or heaven forbid, a hurricane. The sky has gotten even darker during the time we've been talking. If I find out anything, I'll give you a call."

Kelly stood up and hugged Carola. Even though she had one of the most positive attitudes of anyone Kelly had ever met, the threat of her husband possibly being arrested as a suspect in Dudley's murder might be the reason she had dark circles under her eyes. She hadn't said anything, but Kelly wondered if she'd gotten any sleep the night before. "Carola, I don't know who killed Dudley, but rest assured I will do everything I can to clear Jack's name. Okay?"

Tears started to well up in Carola's eyes, and as she wiped them away, she said, "Thank you, Kelly. I've never been through anything like this, and I feel utterly helpless. I really don't know what to do."

"You're doing everything you can, but the most important thing you can do is be there for Jack. He might seem like a guy without a care in the world, but something like this is bound to eat away at him. We've got to clear his name, and we will."

"Thank you again for everything you are doing for both me and Jack," she said as she walked out the door and down the steps.

Kelly looked out at the ocean and the gathering clouds. I don't like this, she thought, *every antenna I have is giving me a resounding high alert. I hope it's nothing.* She turned on the television set and found an English language weather channel which was talking about the coming storm, now predicted to be a category one hurricane with winds from seventy-five miles an hour and up. While some damage was predicted, it was not expected to be major. It was bound for the southerly coast of Cuba. *Oh swell, it's headed exactly towards where we are. Cayo Largo is sixty miles off the south coast of Cuba, so it will hit us first before it makes landfall on Cuba.*

While she was thinking about what she should do, the room phone rang. "Hi, it's me," Carola said. "I just talked to the front desk, and they told me they're expecting a category one hurricane to hit tomorrow. They think we'll be fine because stronger ones have hit this area in the past with only minor damage, but we'll probably have some power outages tomorrow morning. They suggested that Jack not go fishing in the morning, but knowing him, that advice will probably fall on deaf ears. A taxi just pulled up, and I can see Jack. Let's meet in the bar at 7:00. Any chance Mike will be able to join us tonight?"

"I have no idea. I haven't heard from him this afternoon. If I do I'll let you know, otherwise I'll see you at 7:00."

CHAPTER TWENTY-ONE

Kelly picked up the ringing phone. "Hello," she said.

"Hi, sweetheart, it's me. How was your day?"

"It was interesting. I have to tell you that lobster lunch is right up there as one of the top meals of my life. Did you enjoy it as much as I did?"

"Not only enjoyed it, I suffered from overeating almost all afternoon. We've been on the phone and the computer trying to find out more about everyone. Fortunately, Jack checked out very clean. Francisco, the constable, was very impressed with what he found out about him. I think I told you I was going to let him do the research on Jack. I didn't want there to be any sense of impropriety on my part because I came to Cuba with him. As far as Dudley and his wife, they're a rather interesting couple."

"Yes, I did a little research too, because I was curious."

There was a pregnant pause on the other end of the phone and then Mike said, "Kelly..." She interrupted him.

"Mike, it's not what you think. The only thing I've done is look on the computer for some of the people that might be involved, because I've been curious about them."

"Uh-huh, and would I be out of line to ask what conclusions you've drawn?"

"Of course not," Kelly said. "Here's how I read it. I think the three most viable suspects are Philip, Stewart, and Dudley's wife, Patricia. Certainly from what I saw and what you told me Patricia and Stewart would love to have Dudley out of the way, so he's no longer an obstacle to their romantic affair. From what I've read, they've been in love for a long time. Then of course, there's Philip. There is something so off about him."

"I agree, but I can't put my finger on exactly what it is," Mike replied.

"Nor can I," Kelly said, "but there are a number of things that bother me, and they just don't add up. First there's his family life, which seems very sad, and I hate to say it, but from all appearances it looks like he's abandoned his wife in her hour of need. Secondly, from what you've said, it appears that he's bleeding her bank account dry and depositing those funds into an account in his name in the Cayman Islands. That smells. Then there's the fact I've never seen him at dinner since we've been here. I've seen him get two glasses of ice in the bar and then leave. I'm curious why he's getting two glasses of ice. Does he have someone in his room? And where is he eating? You say you've seen him at breakfast, but that's it.

"All the other fishermen want to tell war stories and brag about their day, so they all congregate together before the dinner hour but not Philip. And lastly, what about taking over Dudley's group of fishermen and having those cheesy business cards made? Hate to say it, but he would be real high on my list of possible suspects."

"It almost kills me to say this, Kelly, and please pretend like you never heard it from me, but I value your insights, and I have to tell you I think you may be on to something. Maybe I'd better look at Philip a little closer. I've been looking at Stewart and Patricia, primarily Stewart. Maybe I just don't want to see some American like Philip committing murder on the off chance he can get an exclusive contract to fish in the waters surrounding Cayo Largo. Gotta go, sweetheart, Francisco's motioning to me. Don't know what's happening. I'll probably be late. Go ahead and eat without me."

"Will do. Be careful. Carola told me the front desk told her a category one hurricane is on its way. I love you." She hung up the phone and turned to Cayo, "Well, guess this goes with being married to someone in law enforcement." He answered her by lifting up his head and purring, but a few moments later he was fast asleep. Meanwhile, Kelly listened to the whistling of the wind as its intensity seemed to increase with every passing minute.

CHAPTER TWENTY-TWO

As Kelly and Carola had discussed earlier, the three of them, Kelly, Jack, and Carola met in the bar at 7:00. After they'd seated themselves at a table, Kelly said, "Jack, Mike just called, and it looks like you passed the litmus test, and you're no longer a suspect in Dudley's murder. Seems like the only thing the constable could find on you was simply being in the wrong place at the wrong time, the wrong place being the ocean at the time Dudley was murdered."

"That's a relief," Jack said. "I mean, I know I didn't do anything wrong, and I've never been arrested for anything, but there's always the chance that law enforcement will find something they don't like, and I'd end up in jail. I definitely don't want to find out what the inside of a Cuban jail looks like."

"Don't blame you. Looks like there's going to be some weather tomorrow. Are you planning on going fishing?"

"Yes. My guide said they fish in all kinds of weather, and unless it's a category two hurricane or more, I'll be going out. I'm assuming Mike won't be able to join me again. Correct?"

"That's right. He said the constable has pretty much narrowed it down to three people, and he and the constable will be continuing their investigation during most of the day tomorrow."

Jack turned and said, "Hi, Philip. I thought I heard your voice. Hear you qualified for the Grand Slam Club today."

"Yeah, I've really been lucky," Philip said as he stood next to their table. "It was an awesome experience out there today. Definitely have to put that in my diary. Don't see too many fish like those. The pictures the guide took of me turned out great. Got to add them to my Facebook page and maybe even have a new business card made with a picture of one of the fish on it or maybe all three, since it's representative of fishing in Cuba. By the way, Jack, I'd like to talk to you when we get back to the States about becoming partners in this Cuban fishing thing.

"I've got a lot of ties in the Florida Keys, and I know you're the number one guide whose name appears when anyone searches for fly fishing on the Internet. Since all the fishing here at Cayo Largo is fly fishing, I think we could work really well together as a team. I'll give you a call when we get back. Now that Dudley isn't around, looks like it's just you and me competing for the Bartolo contract. We might as well join forces. What's the old saying? Something about when we're united we stand stronger. Anyway, you know what I mean. Looking forward to fishing with you tomorrow," he said as he walked away from their table.

Jack looked at Kelly and Carola. "That guy is really a good fisherman. Maybe I should join forces with him. He could have the East Coast, and I could have the West Coast."

"Don't even think about it," Carola said. "Something about that guy is downright oily. I don't trust him as far as I could throw him."

"Ditto," Kelly said.

"What are you talking about?" Jack asked. "Do the two of you know something I don't?"

"Maybe, maybe not," Kelly said wiggling the palm of her hand back and forth. "Let's put it this way. There is nothing he can bring to your plate but heartburn, and that you don't need."

"I have no idea what you mean," he said as he stood up. "I'll be back in a minute. I need to visit the men's room and then let's eat. Fishing all day in this heat and humidity really tires me out."

As soon as Jack was out of earshot, Carola leaned toward Kelly and said, "Did you hear Philip say he kept a diary? I would love to see what's in it. I wonder how we could go about getting a quick peek at it."

"That thought occurred to me as soon as the word diary came out of his mouth. I know tomorrow is supposed to bring some bad weather, but with Mike helping the constable and Jack and Philip out fishing, maybe we can find a way to get into his room. Have you developed a relationship with any of the maids?"

"I've talked to the one who's cleaned our room the last couple of mornings, but I have no idea where Philip's room is, or if she cleans his room. What do you have in mind?"

"I'm just wondering if there's any way we can get into his room and look at that diary. If we could find something in it, maybe it would be enough for the constable to arrest him and charge him with murder."

"I'll ask our maid. I'm sure there are strict rules about something like that, but it's been my experience people are often willing to help, particularly if money's involved."

"You think she would take a bribe?" Kelly asked.

"I have no idea, but it wouldn't hurt to have some Cuban money on hand in case she's interested. She and I did talk about money, and I found out she doesn't make much. Having a little extra cash with no questions asked might interest her."

"Jack's almost here. Let's meet in my room at 8:30 tomorrow morning and figure out what we're going to do." She looked up as Jack walked towards them and said, "Hi, Jack. I'm ready to eat. Let's go see what terrific things they have for us at the buffet tonight."

CHAPTER TWENTY-THREE

Kelly tossed and turned all night, listening to the wind and just before dawn, she heard the sound of rain over the hum of the air conditioner. Mike left at 7:30 for breakfast and to meet Francisco. After he left she got up and opened the drapes. The trees were swaying back and forth in the strong winds, and rain pelted against the windows. The sea looked angry.

She quickly dressed and hurried down to the restaurant. It was filled with people needing their morning jolt of caffeine, but unlike every other morning, no one was seated at a window table. The servers had taken the linens off of those tables due to the slanting wind-driven rain which had covered them with rainwater. *"Hola,"* Kelly said to the server whose area of the restaurant she had been seated in for the last few days. *"Café, por favor."* A moment later the server set a hot cup of coffee in front of her. In broken English she said, "We have much rain. It will last all day and get bad about noon, but we will be okay. Do not worry."

"Gracias," Kelly said inwardly thinking that it was easy for the server to say not to worry, but she was definitely worried. She took a napkin from the table and walked over to the buffet, put some sausage and scrambled eggs on a plate, and then stood near the restaurant entrance, dreading the walk back to her room. Cayo had made his rounds, but evidently he'd been watching her, because as soon as she walked out of the building into the rain, he was right

beside her. She was glad someone had thought to put an umbrella in her room, and she gratefully opened it as she hurried back to the room. Although it was almost 8:30 in the morning, the sky was very dark. She shivered and couldn't decide whether it was from the unusual quiet or a sense of foreboding. Usually whenever she walked out of her room she could hear music playing and the lilting voices of the workers talking to one another echoing across the hotel grounds. Not this morning.

Kelly had barely closed the door when there was a knock on it. "Who is it?" she asked. She knew it was probably Carola, but Mike had made it very clear she was never to open a door without knowing who was on the other side.

"It's me, Kelly, open up. I'm beginning to feel like a drowned rat out here."

Carola walked in, leaving her umbrella on the porch outside the room. "I don't know who had the foresight to put that in my room, but I'll be forever indebted to them. This is horrible. I didn't bring a raincoat, but even if I had I wouldn't have worn it, because it's too hot and humid for one. And from what they told me at the front desk this morning, it's going to be a little worse than they thought."

"That's just great. Now what?"

"I called the front desk last night after dinner when Jack was taking a shower and asked them if I could have my room cleaned at 7:30 this morning. They said that would be fine. Shortly after Jack left for breakfast and fishing, the maid I've spoken with several times came to the room to clean it. I made small talk with her, and then I told her I had a problem. I said I was sure she was a woman who understood that sometimes a man and a woman are attracted to each other outside of one's marriage. I told her there was a man I was very attracted to, and I would like to surprise him by going into his room and waiting for him, but I couldn't let my husband or anyone else know. I asked her if I gave her the number of a room if she could let me into it. I could tell she didn't want to do it, so I took a hundred peso Cuban bill out of my money belt and put it on the table next to where we were talking. I saw her eyes keep straying to it. I never said anything. She became very quiet, and then she told me if I would give her the bill she would do it."

"Carola, that's brilliant. I just hope this thing doesn't backfire. I don't think Jack would be very happy with you."

"I'm sure he wouldn't, but if it saves his career and helps catch Dudley's killer, I'm sure he'll overlook it. I also called the front desk last night and found out that Philip's room number is 2706. My maid is meeting us there at 9:00, so we probably need to try and find it. I'm not looking forward to going out in the rain again and then stumbling around trying to find his room. I couldn't find my site map of the resort anywhere."

"You won't have to. I've still got mine. Just a minute." After a quick search of her suitcase Kelly said, "Here it is." She looked at it for a moment. "Actually, we won't have to walk far at all. His room is only two buildings away. Carola, you're going to think I'm nuts, but when we were researching what to bring to Cuba, Mike read that we should bring some small plastic bags." While she was speaking she pulled four plastic bags out of her suitcase. "I know this sounds strange, but when we search Philip's room for the diary, we should both put our hands in these plastic bags. That way, if something goes really wrong, they won't find our fingerprints on anything."

"Kelly, you probably are nuts, but it's a brilliant idea. I'm ready to go when you are. I'd like to get this over with."

"Me, too. I don't technically think this qualifies as breaking and entering, but I really don't want to find out if my semantics are off when I talk to the Cuban constable. To say nothing of the fact that Mike would be furious if his wife was arrested for breaking and entering when he's working with the constable to solve a capital crime. No, that definitely would not be a good thing." She opened the door to a sheet of blinding rain as they both stepped out into the fury of the ever increasing storm.

CHAPTER TWENTY-FOUR

Kelly and Carola hurried down the path to the building where Philip's room was located. As usual, Cayo tagged right along next to them. They saw the maid's cart next to the building sheltered by an overhang. "Kelly, I better go by myself, and you can come in when you see the maid leave. She might think it's a little over the top for two women to be meeting Philip. With our age difference, it would kind of look like a mother-daughter thing, and that might be beyond the scope of believability."

"Why don't you stand under the overhang of the building next door? You'll be out of the rain, and there's no one around, so I don't think anyone will question why you're standing there. I brought a flashlight for two reasons. One, I doubt that Philip has made friends with the people in the nearby rooms, but I'd rather people didn't see lights on in his room if they know he's gone. Secondly, there will probably be a power outage at some point today, and I wanted to be prepared. Wish me luck." She blew a kiss to Kelly, and with that she walked towards Philip's room. The maid opened the door when she knocked and let her in. A few minutes later Kelly saw the maid leave the room and walk down the path, a clear plastic tarp covering her head and her cleaning equipment.

Kelly hurried over to the room she'd seen Carola enter and knocked. *If I've got the wrong room, this could get real interesting,* she thought. *I could always say I became confused because of the darkness and the rain.* Fortunately Carola opened the door and Kelly and Cayo walked in.

"Kelly, I've never done anything like this, and I don't have a clue where to start."

"Start by putting one of the plastic bags we brought on each of your hands. I hope you remembered not to touch anything in the room after the maid let you in. Why don't you take the bedroom, and I'll take his closet and bathroom? We're looking primarily for the diary, but if you find something else of interest, take it. Of course the bad news is that we don't know if he meant he wrote in his diary when he was here, or whether he kept one at home. Let's hope for the best."

They were both quiet for a few minutes as they started searching the room and then Carola said, "Kelly, I found something interesting. His iPad is here, and I turned it on. You can't access the Internet from the rooms, but the iPad opens to the last place the person using it was reading. It looks like he's copied and pasted information about calcium chloride. I don't know what this means, but I think we should take it and show it to Mike."

"I agree, but I may hide it for a few days. I know Mike would definitely not approve of what we're doing at the moment. Let's keep looking for the diary, but yes, that is very, very interesting. Why would he have information on his iPad about calcium chloride? I don't even know what it is."

"Carola, I found it," Kelly said about fifteen minutes later. "Let's go to my room, I'm really uncomfortable here. I read that the Santeria religion is practiced here in Cuba with juju and stuff like that, and right now, I'm feeling a lot of really bad energy or juju. I just want to get out of here."

They quickly glanced around to make sure nothing had been disturbed. "Carola, I just thought of something. You got the maid to let us in, so we could find this stuff. Now we're leaving. Question is, how do we get back in if we need to replace the iPad and the diary?"

"I have no idea. Let's just hope it's not necessary. We'll cross that bridge when we come to it. We can talk about it once we look at the diary."

They looked around the room one final time and decided it didn't look like anyone had been in the room other than the maid. Kelly opened the door and peered out from side to side. "Coast is clear, let's go. Cayo, come." Moments later they were back in Kelly's room, out of the rain, the diary in front of them.

"What do you think's in it?" Kelly asked. "Maybe it's nothing more than him recording thoughts he has like maybe his shrink or someone told him to do."

"I have no idea, but let's find out."

They both put plastic bags back on their hands. "You do it, Kelly. I really don't know what to look for."

"Well, if it's any consolation, I'm not so sure I do either." She began leafing through the diary. "From what I'm seeing, he must keep a separate one for each year. Obviously, this one is for this year."

"And?" Carola asked.

"I'm looking for the entries he made last week. I think that's what would be relevant. Give me a couple of minutes." She was quiet for several minutes and then said, "I think we just hit the mother lode."

"What do you mean?"

"Last week he wrote he was going to Cuba and was going to see what he could do to become the United States go-to person for fishing in Cuba. From that day forward he lists the people he's met, how they can help him get an exclusive contract to represent Americans wanting to fish in Cuba, and there's a large section devoted to Dudley. Oh, Carola, I don't believe this," she said, her breath catching.

"What did you find?" Carola asked.

"He says it was necessary to kill Dudley, because after he caught the bonefish, the tarpon, and the permit, and was eligible to become a member of the Grand Slam Club, he had to die. Philip wrote that if Dudley became the only English guide to ever do that he would almost certainly get the contract from Bartolo. That would mean he would have the exclusive rights to Europe as well as the United States, and he couldn't allow that to happen."

"I knew something was wrong with him!" Carola exclaimed.

"Philip writes that his doctor gave him a prescription for calcium chloride, because he's prone to muscle spasms. Evidently the doctor told him to be very careful if he gave himself an injection, because an overdose could cause his heart to stop beating. He says he was glad he remembered what the doctor told him, and he used a huge injection of calcium chloride to kill Dudley. He says the information he got on the Internet when he used his iPad indicated an overdose of calcium chloride was practically impossible to trace."

She continued reading. "Carola, he's written that last night when they were in the taxi coming back from the marina he asked Jack if he could fish with him today. He said Jack needed to have a bad accident, and that way he could become the exclusive representative for Bartolo. He says Jack is his final competitor for the fishing rights, and he needs to be eliminated."

"Kelly, that means he's out in the boat with Jack right now and in this weather! He could do something to Jack and make it look like it was a weather-related accident.

"Jack told me when they left the fishing club yesterday Philip told Guido he wanted to fish with Jack today, and they wouldn't need a Cuban guide. Philip said he wanted to work for Jack if Jack got the Bartolo contract, and he wanted to show him what a good guide he could be. He said he's been here several times, so he knows how to run the boat, and they would fish in the zone closest to the marina."

Carola looked at Kelly with a terrified look of fright on her face as she slowly realized the enormity of the extreme danger Jack must be in at that very moment. The increasing fury of the howling wind and the rain pelting against the window didn't help her fright, it only increased it. Kelly made an instant decision and said, "Carola, you're the one who speaks fluent Spanish. Go to the front desk, and tell them you need to speak to the constable immediately. Tell Mike what we've found out and tell him that the constable and Mike need to get to the marina as fast as they can."

"What are you going to do?"

Kelly pulled a lightweight raincoat over her head and said, "I'm going to the fishing club and get Guido to take me out to where Philip said they were going to fish today. Pray we're in time." Cayo sensed something was happening and jumped into the beach bag Kelly was carrying. She ran out the door and down the steps leading from her room, intent on getting someone to take her to the marina.

CHAPTER TWENTY-FIVE

Kelly ran through the lobby and over to where the security guard was standing. "I need a taxi! Right now!"

"I'm sorry, *senora*, one just left and there are only two on the island. It will be perhaps half an hour before another one will be here."

She frantically looked around and saw a man getting into a maintenance truck with the logo *"Compania Electrica de Cayo Largo"* written on the side. Kelly ran over to him. *"Senor,* if you can take me to the marina, I will pay you well. Please, this is an emergency."

The man looked blankly at her, evidently not understanding a word she'd said. The burly Cuban security guard had followed her and translated what she'd said. He told the man it was an emergency.

The guard turned to Kelly. "He wants to know what kind of an emergency."

"A friend of mine is going to be killed, if I don't get there immediately. Please, tell him someone's life is in his hands. I have one hundred Cuban pesos for him if he will take me there."

The guard spoke rapidly to the man. The mention of money seemed to make the difference. He spoke to the guard who opened the front door for Kelly. "Get in. Where do you want him to take you?"

"I want to go to the Bartolo fishing club at the marina. The Grand Slam Club. Can he take me there?"

Again the guard spoke rapidly in Spanish and turned back to Kelly. "He knows where it is and will have you there in a few minutes." He closed the door, and the driver pulled out onto the road. Between the rain and the darkness it was almost impossible to see anything, but after a few minutes the man pulled into the parking lot of the building Kelly had visited a few days earlier and pointed to the building.

"*Gracias,*" she said throwing the door open and giving him a one hundred peso bill. "*Vaya con Dios,*" the man said, "Go with God."

Believe me, I hope he's with me, she thought as she burst through the fishing club's door and saw Guido sitting at his desk.

"*Senora* Reynolds, what are you doing here on such a miserable day? You should be at the hotel, waiting out the hurricane."

"I don't have time to tell you. I need you to take me to where Philip and Jack are fishing. I know Philip told you he didn't need a guide today, and that he and Jack would go out by themselves. You must know where they are. You have to take me there immediately, and if you have a gun, bring it. My husband and the constable will be coming shortly."

"*Senora*, I don't have authority..."

Kelly cut him off. "You better assume whatever authority you need, because if you don't Jack is going to be murdered and even if you're not charged with being an accomplice to murder, I'll make sure that everyone knows you had a chance to save a client's life and didn't. If that happens, I don't think you'll need to worry about assuming authority, because I'll bet you will no longer be employed as the head fishing guide here."

Guido hesitated for a moment and then reached into the bottom drawer of his desk and took a gun from it. "Follow me. My boat is tied up at the dock." He pulled a raincoat over his head and put on a rain hat. They ran through the courtyard and down to the dock. He quickly untied the rope securing the boat to the dock and started the boat's motor. "Sit behind me," he said as he stood at the steering wheel and sped away from the dock. "All of our boats are equipped with a GPS system, so I can tell where each boat is located at all times. I can locate their boat using the GPS. It will take me a moment, but I'll head in the general direction where I think they are and soon the GPS will show me exactly where their boat is. It's accurate to a distance of ten meters."

Kelly set her beach bag down on the floor of the boat and was surprised at how heavy it was. She hadn't been aware of it on her way to the marina. She looked down and saw two eyes looking up at her. *Good grief, I completely forgot about Cayo. Poor thing must be terrified to be in a boat and on the water.*

"*Senora*, I have found their boat's location on the GPS. It's not too far from here."

"Guido, when we pulled away from the dock I noticed there weren't any other boats around. I think you met Jack's wife, Carola. She's calling my husband, who's a sheriff, and the constable, but how will they find us without a boat?"

"The constable has his own boat at the marina, and there is a radio on his boat. He will be able to call me, and I can tell him where we are headed."

"In this weather even with your GPS system, how will you ever be able to find their boat?"

"Each boat is equipped with the best GPS system that is made. It could locate where a fly was if we programmed it for that. Don't worry, we'll get there in time for whatever it is you're worried about. Please, *Senora*, could you tell me what is the problem?"

Kelly spent the next few minutes filling Guido in on what she and Carola had discovered in Philip's diary. She told him when it was all over she would tell him why she'd become suspicious of Philip. Guido slowed the boat down and turned off the engine. She could make out the running lights on a boat that was about fifty yards ahead of them.

Guido looked back at her and said over his shoulder, "That's their boat. Now what do you want me to do?"

"Do you have binoculars on the boat?"

"Yes, they're in the dry storage bin beneath where you're sitting." She stood up, and he pulled the top of the storage bin open and handed her a pair of binoculars. She could make out two figures in the boat and said a silent prayer as it looked like they'd gotten there in time. The wind dropped suddenly, and the water became very calm. Voices carry considerable distances across quiet calm water and she heard Jack ask, "What are you talking about?"

She leaned close to Guido and whispered, "Why did the wind drop?"

"*Senora*, I think we're in the eye of the hurricane. Often it gets very quiet before the torrential rains come."

"So the rains we've been having haven't been torrential?"

"No, *Senora*. In about twenty minutes it will be very bad. What now?"

"Can you quietly pole our boat close to them? I seem to remember you saying that's what the guides did when they got to where they wanted to fish, and with Jack and Philip both looking forward, maybe we can get close to them without being noticed."

"*Si, Senora.* I can do that." They heard angry voices coming from the boat in front of them.

Jack, who was usually very mild-mannered, angrily said in a raised voice, "No, Philip, I don't want to be your partner. The company contacted me, not you, and I have every intention of being their representative in the United States."

"Then you leave me no option. I'll have to kill you just like I killed Dudley. I was afraid that's what you'd say, and that's why I didn't want a Cuban guide to come with us today. I'll tell everyone you fell overboard, and even though the water is shallow, it was raining so hard, and it was so dark, I couldn't find you. By the time your body washes up on shore, the fish will have had their share of you, and it's very hard to determine the cause of death from a body when all that's left are the bones."

"*Senora*, what do you want me to do?" Guido asked in an alarmed tone of voice.

"Get as close as you can to their boat. Get your gun out and be ready to shoot Philip, if need be."

"But *Senora*, he's qualified to become a member of the Grand Slam Club. I can't do that."

"Then hand the gun to me. I have no problem shooting him."

He handed her the gun, as he quietly poled their boat to within ten feet of Jack's boat. Out of the corner of her eye she saw that Cayo had gotten out of her beach bag and had walked up to the bow of the boat.

They were so close to the other boat that Kelly could clearly see Philip reach into a bag at his feet and pull a syringe out of it. "Jack, this won't hurt. It will all be over in a matter of..."

"Cayo," Kelly yelled as the calico cat hissed and leaped the short distance from her boat to Jack's boat. He sprang at Philip, biting him on the neck and clawing through his shirt with enough force to draw blood.

"Don't move, Philip. I have a gun and being married to a sheriff, I know how to use it," Kelly shouted. "Drop the syringe, or I'll shoot." Philip meekly complied and dropped the syringe on the floor of the boat.

"*Senora*, the constable's boat is coming. I'm turning my lights on and starting the engine. We need to get back to shore. I fear the heavy weather will start very soon."

The constable pulled up next to them. "Kelly, Jack," Mike yelled, "Are you all right?"

"Yes," they both answered. Jack continued, "Philip was getting ready to kill me. Kelly saved my life."

"*Senor* Mike, hurry! We don't have time to talk. The worst of the hurricane is coming, and we need to get off the water," Guido said.

"Mike, take my gun and keep it on Philip," the constable said as he pulled Philip over the side of the boat he and Jack had been in and into the constable's boat. "I'll handcuff him. *Senor* Jack, drive your boat back to the dock. Guido, stay right behind us, so if he tries anything either the *Senora* or Mike can shoot him. With two guns on him, I don't expect much trouble. We need to go now!"

The three boats sped back to shore as best they could in the water which was now becoming wild and angry. As they pulled up to the dock, the heavens opened, and the full strength of the hurricane blew over and around them. A terrible roar filled the air. "Follow me, the fishing club is safe," Guido yelled. "It was built with something like this in mind. We will be okay there. Run."

They ran as fast as they could through the deluge of pouring rain, Cayo safely back in Kelly's beach bag. The force of the wind had flung the door of the fishing club open, and the floor was covered with water. Guido yelled to them, "Get in the back room, away from the windows. The wind could blow them out. Stay as far back in the room as you can."

He pushed open the door of the back room, and they huddled on the floor against the back wall. The constable unceremoniously pushed Philip down on the floor and told him to stay there. He pressed his foot on the back of Philip's neck as all of them anxiously waited for the storm to subside. For the next two hours there was silence in the room as the six of them listened to the raging storm and watched the slanting rain pounding against the windows. Kelly and Mike had never been in a hurricane and the two hours they spent huddled on the floor in the back room of the fishing clubhouse felt like a lifetime to them.

"Kelly, Carola stayed at the hotel, right?" Jack asked.

"Yes, and it's fully prepared for hurricanes. I noticed evacuation signs on the grounds, and when I left they were calling people to come to the lobby so they could be evacuated. Don't forget, the hotel is on a cliff, so she should be fine. When I last saw her, she was in the lobby, getting ready to call the constable. I'm sure she's okay, just frightened, like all of us are."

After nearly two hours of enduring the thrashing of the violent storm it became eerily quiet. The rain stopped, and the sun broke through the clouds. "It is over," Guido said. "We are fine, and so is the fishing club."

"*Senor* Mike, would you ride in the car with me?" the constable asked. "I need to take Philip to jail, and then we will fly him to the main island. Thank you so much. You solved the case, or rather, the *Senora* did. *Gracias, Senora.* I don't know what we would have done without you and your cat."

Kelly didn't look at Mike as she answered him. "*De nada*, it was nothing, and he's really not my cat. I was lucky. Who knew Cayo was some sort of a killer attack cat? I'm going to hate to leave him."

"Kelly, Mike, I can never thank you enough, and I have to say that Carola was right," Jack said. "She had a sixth sense about Philip, and I didn't listen. It almost cost me my life. Mike, you haven't even been able to fish which is the main reason you came to Cuba."

"Senors, tomorrow you will go with Landy. He is my best guide. You will fish with him as my guests, without charge," Guido said. "Needless to say, Philip will not be getting the Grand Slam certificate or his photograph on the wall. He is not qualified to become a member of the prestigious Grand Slam Club. He dishonors what so many have come to prize."

"Senor Mike, *Senora* Reynolds, I am so sorry, but could you come to the station and make a statement?" the constable asked. "Mike, you're going to be fishing tomorrow, and I believe you told me you were leaving the day after tomorrow for Havana. I think now is the only time you can do it, plus I would like to have you keep my gun on Philip while I take him to jail. We have so little crime on the island that I don't have a deputy. I need to arrange for Philip to be taken to Havana and charged with murder. Your statements will be indispensable."

"Of course," Mike said. "Kelly that's all right with you, isn't it?"

"Yes, but when we get back to the hotel, I want to get a special treat for Cayo. He's the one who should get the credit of thwarting a murder. I know dogs are protective, but cats? That's something I never knew. He's an island cat and part of the flavor here, but I'm really going to miss him."

"I know what you're thinking, Kelly," Mike said, "and the answer is no. We have two dogs, one of which was given to us, and more or less under protest I agreed to take her. We are definitely not going to add any more pets to our menagerie."

"Constable, do you have any sway with the taxis on the island? I know you need to get Philip to jail, and Guido has business here at the clubhouse, but I sure would like to get back to the hotel and see if Carola's all right," Jack said.

The constable picked up his phone, punched a number in, and said something rapidly in Spanish. He turned to Jack, "The taxi will be here momentarily. When the constable asks the taxi driver to do something, it takes precedence over his paying customers. I'll call your hotel and make sure all is well there, and everyone survived safely." After another conversation in rapid Spanish, he said, "Everything is fine. I told them to call your room and tell your wife that you are all right. The hotel escaped damage, and about the only thing that happened was some of the guests got wet. All in all, I guess one could call that a successful hurricane."

As soon as they arrived at the constable's office and Philip was safely locked behind bars in the only jail cell in the building, the constable said, "Please, give me one minute. I need to call headquarters in Havana and ask them to send a couple of men out on the early afternoon plane. That way they can take him back on the evening plane. If he stays here, I may not be responsible for what I might do to him. We regard our fishing opportunities very highly, and to think that a man who could have possibly become a member of the Grand Slam Club did something like what *Senor* Montgomery did is simply a slap in the face to all of us."

When they got back to their hotel room after giving their statements to the constable, Mike said, "Kelly, I didn't want to say anything in front of the constable, but paying a chambermaid to get into someone's room and searching his room? If you were in the United States you could be arrested for trespassing, as well as breaking and entering."

"That's not true. There was no breaking and entering or trespassing. Who says there was? Certainly not the constable. I've always kind of gone along with what Machiavelli said in his famous book, 'The Prince,' about the ends justifying the means, and in this case Jack's alive. That's what's important."

Mike looked at her and shook his head.

They spent the rest of the afternoon enjoying the beautiful Caribbean beach which had been magically restored with no remnants from the violent hurricane other than where the ocean had crept up on the shore at the height of its intensity.

CHAPTER TWENTY-SIX

At 10:00 the next morning Kelly went down to breakfast, intent on eating everything she could that was Cuban. It was a strange breakfast, but she knew it was one of her last in Cuba, and certainly the only one where she would be able to sample whatever she wanted. They were leaving on the first plane out the following day, so they could spend the day exploring Havana.

Albondigas meatballs, Spanish sausages, mango juice, several different kinds of breads and cookies, Spanish bacon, garbanzo beans, and chicken with rice. She took a little of everything that interested her. Kelly had just sat down when she felt a tap on her shoulder. "Good morning," Carola said. "I was going to suggest going down to the beach for a little while and then taking a siesta, but looking at that plate, I'm not sure you're going to be able to move after you eat all that's on it."

"I know. I think my eyes were bigger than my stomach which is one reason why I try to avoid buffets. I always take a little of this and a little of that, and I can never eat all of it, but since this is our last day here, I'd love to join you on the beach. Have you eaten yet?"

"Yes, I ate with Mike and Jack. They were both excited to get back on the water. Poor Mike. He paid all that money to come down here and then barely got to fish. I hope he does well today."

"So do I," Kelly said. "He loves to fish, but he's not what he calls 'pole obsessed' like Philip. You know I've never met Philip's wife, but I feel sorry for her. Cancer, an infant, and now her husband will be going to a Cuban prison for a long, long time. What a thing for that poor child. I hope Philip's parents do a better job with their grandson than they did with him. Anyway, why don't I meet you in the lobby at 10:30, and we can spend some time on the beach? If the humidity gets to me, I can always go back to the room."

"See you then," Carola said, blowing kisses to the hotel employees as she left the room.

Three hours later, Kelly turned to Carola and said, "I feel like I'm a wet piece of putty. I'm heading back to the room. Let's meet for a drink in the bar at 7:00."

"Sounds great. I think I'll go back to the room and take a little siesta. See you at 7:00."

*****

Kelly fell asleep with Cayo lying next to her on the bed. When she woke up she thought, *I'm not so sure that was a good idea, and I'm not so sure the hotel would be very happy about guests bringing stray cats into their rooms, but what the heck. If it hadn't been for Cayo, I'm not sure Jack would be alive.*

She got out of bed and took a shower, knowing that the first thing Mike was going to want to do when he returned from fishing was wash off the salt spray from the boat trip and also rinse his clothing out in the shower. Jack had been very emphatic that if you've been out fishing in a boat all day the first thing you do when you get back to your room is get in the shower with your clothes on, and when they're completely wet, throw them in the sink and wash the salt spray off of your body. After your shower, hang the wet clothes out on the balcony, so they'll be dry, salt free, and ready to wear the next day. Kelly finished up in the bathroom, knowing Mike would command it when he got back.

A few minutes later there was a knock on the door. "Who is it?" Kelly asked.

"It's me, Mike. Open up. This may be the most exciting day of my life."

"Okay, I'll bite," she said as she opened the door. "You went fishing. I can only assume you got a fish, maybe a couple."

He picked her up and swung her around. "No, I not only got a fish. I got three fish. Kelly, you are now looking at an official member of the exclusive Grand Slam Club. Look, here's the certificate. Guido gave it to me himself as a thank you for everything I've done. This may be the most thrilling thing that's ever happened to me."

"Careful, Sheriff. Thought you already said that on the day we were married."

"Okay, you got me. Let's just say it's on par with that day. They photographed me, and my picture is going to be on the wall at the Bartolo clubhouse. I mean, people from all over the world will know that Mike Reynolds is now a member of the Grand Slam Club. I can't believe it."

"What about Jack?" Kelly asked.

"He got five bonefish and three tarpon."

"Well, that seems pretty impressive to me."

"Normally, it would be very impressive, but here's the thing. I only got three fish, but they were the ones that count, the tarpon, the permit, and the bonefish. Actually, Jack is thrilled for me."

"Really? I'd think he'd be a little jealous."

"Not at all. Look at it this way. I'm a paying customer. He takes me on his first trip to Cuba, and his client qualifies to become a member of the prestigious Grand Slam Club. That constitutes some pretty big bragging rights, not only for me, but for Jack as well."

"Yeah, I see what you mean. Go take a shower and try to come down from the planet you're on. We're meeting them in the bar at 7:00. You've got an hour."

"Kelly, I don't think you're giving me the respect I'm due for having accomplished this remarkable feat," Mike said with a twinkle in his eyes.

"Sheriff, think it's one of those 'had to be there things,' and I wasn't there, although I am sorry I wasn't. I'm sure it was really exciting."

"Beyond," he said, as he walked into the bathroom.

*****

Promptly at 7:00 they walked into the open-air bar and saw Jack waving to them. In front of him was a bottle of champagne with four glass flutes. "Kelly, Mike, we're celebrating. It doesn't get much better than this, a murder solved and my client getting a grand slam on my first guiding trip in Cuba. Who knew when we left the United States that all this would take place. Not me!"

"Jack, I'm going to speak for both of us," Kelly said. "Yes, there was a murder and that always saddens me, but we're all safe, Mike is now a member of the Grand Slam Club, and we had the best lobster of our lives on the beach at Playa Sirena. I will never forget that, and I rather doubt anyone else will either. You did a good job, Mr. Fly Fishing Guide."

"Thanks, but believe me, I had no idea all this would take place when I called to see if you'd be interested in coming to Cuba with me."

"My friend, I wouldn't have missed it for the world. Thanks for the invite. Tomorrow we fly to Havana and the next day to Mexico

City and then home. Problem is, I think I need a vacation from this vacation," Mike said laughing as each of them held up their glass of champagne and toasted Mike and the trip.

*****

The next morning while they were packing, Kelly said, "I think Cayo knows we're leaving, and he's sad. I wish I could take him with us."

"No, Kelly, the answer is a resounding NO. Two dogs are enough, plus Cayo has a major job here at the resort keeping the mice at bay. Think what might happen to this resort if he wasn't around to do it. It's kind of like some higher being decided to lend him to us for a little while, and he certainly did what was needed at a crucial time. And believe me, sweetheart, I, for one, am very grateful."

"Mike, I rather doubt Jack would be alive if it wasn't for Cayo. I know the van will be here in a little while, but I'm going down to the buffet and prepare a plate of food for my feline friend Cayo that includes everything a cat would like. See you in the lobby in a half hour."

Kelly walked into the lobby area with a very satisfied Cayo walking next to her. "Looks like the van's here, and I see Carola and Jack coming," she said to Mike. She stooped down and petted Cayo. "Bye little guy. Thanks for everything." She stood up and looked down at him, sure that the reflection shining in his eyes was simply a reflection of the unshed tears she had in her eyes.

"*Vaya con Dios*, little friend," She followed Mike, Jack, and Carola into the van as the staff smiled and waved their goodbyes.

RECIPES

ARROZ CON POLLO (RICE WITH CHICKEN)

Ingredients

4 skinless, boneless chicken breast halves
½ tsp. salt
½ tsp. freshly ground black pepper
½ tsp. paprika
3 tbsp. vegetable oil
1 green bell pepper, chopped
¾ cup chopped onion
1 ½ tsps. minced garlic
1 cup long-grain white rice
1 (14.5 oz.) can chicken broth
½ cup white wine
1/8 tsp. saffron
1 (14.5 oz.) can stewed tomatoes
1 tbsp. chopped fresh parsley

Directions

Cut chicken breasts into 1 inch pieces and sprinkle with ¼ tsp. each of salt, pepper, and paprika. Heat oil in a large skillet over medium heat. Add chicken, turning, and cooking until golden. Remove chicken and set aside.

Add green pepper, onions, and garlic to skillet. Cook for 5 minutes. Add rice and cook until rice is opaque, 1 – 2 minutes. Stir in chicken broth, wine, saffron, tomatoes, remaining salt, pepper, and paprika. Bring to a boil. Cover and lower temperature to simmer. Cook for 20 minutes.

Return chicken to pan until reheated. Stir in parsley. Serve and enjoy!

ARROZ CON LECHE (RICE WITH MILD - PUDDING)

Ingredients

2 ¾ cups water
1 ½ cups short grained rice
1 (1/4 inch x 3 inch) strip lime peel
1 cinnamon stick
2 tbsp. anise seed, crushed
1 (12 oz.) can evaporated milk
1 (14 oz.) can condensed milk
1 tbsp. vanilla extract
1/3 tsp. salt
¾ cup raisins, optional

Directions

Combine 2 ¼ cups of water, rice, and lime peel in a saucepan. Bring to boil over medium-high heat, then reduce heat to medium-low, cover, and simmer for 20 minutes until rice is tender. While the rice is cooking, combine ½ cup water, cinnamon stick, and anise in another saucepan over medium-high heat. Bring mixture to a low boil for 3 minutes, then remove saucepan from heat.

When rice is finished cooking, reduce heat to low, remove the lime peel with a slotted spoon, and gradually add evaporated milk and condensed milk into the rice. Add the cinnamon and anise flavored water, vanilla, salt, and raisins, if desired. Continue to stir until the mixture thickens, about 7 – 10 minutes. If the pudding is too watery after 10 minutes, turn up heat to medium-low and stir continuously until it reaches desired consistency. Remove from heat and pour into individual dishes. Refrigerate until fully chilled and ready to serve. Enjoy!

ALBONDIGAS (CUBAN MEATBALLS) IN SAUCE

Meatballs Ingredients

2 eggs
1 cup cracker crumbs (I use packaged)
¼ cup milk
1 ½ lbs. ground beef
1 tsp. dry yellow mustard
2 tsp. cumin
½ tsp. pepper
1 small onion, chopped
½ green onion, finely chopped
1 tbsp. olive oil
Flour for coating meatballs

Sauce Ingredients

2 tbsp. olive oil
1 medium onion, chopped
1 green pepper, chopped
4 garlic cloves, mashed
1/3 cup ketchup
1 tbsp. white vinegar
1 tbsp. brown sugar
1 tsp. salt
1 (15 oz.) can tomato sauce

Directions

In a large bowl, combine eggs, cracker crumbs, and milk. Blend in the ground beef and remaining ingredients. (I use my hands to mix it.) Form into balls about 2 inches in diameter. Lightly roll meatballs in flour. Heat olive oil over medium-high heat and add meatballs to oil. Cook 3 – 5 minutes turning so all sides are browned. When fully cooked remove from oil and drain on a paper towel lined cookie sheet.

To make sauce, sauté onion and green pepper in olive oil until translucent. Add mashed garlic during the last minute or two of frying. Remove garlic. Add remaining ingredients and mix well. Pour sauce into a large sauce pan, add the meatballs, and bring mixture to a boil. Reduce heat and simmer on low for about 30 minutes. To serve, remove meatballs to a serving platter, topped with desired amount of sauce. Enjoy!

TRES LECHES CAKE (CAKE WITH THREE KINDS OF MILK)

Cake Ingredients

1 cup sugar, divided
5 large eggs, separated and at room temperature
1/3 cup milk
½ teaspoon vanilla extract
1 cup flour, sifted
1 ½ tsp. baking powder
½ tsp. cream of tartar

Directions

Preheat oven to 350 degrees. Butter a 9 x 13 inch pan. In a large mixing bowl beat ¾ cup sugar and 5 egg yolks for approximately 5 minutes or until the yolks are pale yellow. Gently stir in the milk, vanilla extract, flour, and baking powder.

In another bowl, beat the 5 egg whites until soft peaks form, adding the cream of tartar after 20 seconds. Gradually add the remaining ¼ cup sugar and continue beating until the whites are glossy and firm. Gently fold the egg white mixture into the egg yolk mixture. Pour the batter into a baking dish and bake 40 – 50 minutes or until a toothpick inserted in the center comes out clean. Remove from oven and let cake cool completely on a metal rack. While the cake is cooling, prepare the syrup.

Syrup Ingredients

1 (12 oz.) can evaporated milk
1 cup sweetened condensed milk
1 cup whipping cream
1 tsp. vanilla extract
1 tbsp. dark Cuban rum

Directions

In a large bowl combine the ingredients until well blended.

When the cake has cooled, pierce it about every ½ inch, taking care not to tear the cake. Keep the cake in the baking dish and place it on a rimmed baking sheet to catch the syrup when it overflows. Slowly pour the syrup over the top of the cake, spooning the overflow back on top until all the syrup is absorbed.

Topping Ingredients

1 cup whipping cream
2 tbsp. granulated sugar
½ tsp. vanilla extract

Directions

In a small mixing bowl, beat the cream, sugar, and vanilla until stiff peaks form. Gently spread over the top of the cake after the syrup has soaked in. Enjoy!

MOROS Y CRISTIANOS (BLACK BEANS AND RICE DISH)

Ingredients

1 ½ cups dried black beans
¼ cup olive oil
2 ½ cups diced onions
2 ½ cups green pepper, seeded and diced
4 cloves garlic, crushed and chopped
3 tsp. ground cumin
1 tsp. oregano
1 bay leaf
3 tbsp. white vinegar
2 tbsp. tomato paste
2 tsp. salt
½ tsp. freshly ground pepper
4 ½ cups chicken stock
3 cups long grain white rice
2 tbsp. chopped parsley or cilantro for garnish

Directions

Cover the dry beans with 4 cups of water in a large saucepan. Bring to a boil for 20 minutes. Remove from heat and let stand covered for one hour.

Drain and rinse the beans. Add enough water to cover them and bring to a boil. Reduce heat to low, cover, and cook until tender, about 45 – 60 minutes. Drain.

Rinse the rice with cold water until the water runs clear. Use a large covered stockpot and sauté the onion and green pepper in the olive oil until tender. Add garlic and sauté 1 – 2 minutes. Add tomato paste, black beans, oregano, cumin, bay leaf, and vinegar. Cook for about five minutes, stirring gently. Add the chicken stock and rice. Bring to a boil, reduce heat to low, cover and cook for about 20 – 30 minutes until rice is fully cooked.

Adjust seasonings by adding salt and pepper to taste. Remove bay leaf and serve. Enjoy!

Amazing Ebooks & Paperbacks for FREE

Go to www.dianneharman.com/freepaperback.html and get your FREE copies of Dianne's books and Dianne's favorite recipes immediately by signing up for her newsletter.

Once you've signed up for her newsletter you're eligible to win autographed paperbacks. One lucky winner is picked every week. Hurry before the offer ends.

ABOUT THE AUTHOR

Dianne lives in Huntington Beach, California with her husband Tom, a former California State Senator, and her boxer puppy, Kelly. Her passions are cooking and dogs, so whenever she has a little free time, you can find her in the kitchen or in the back yard throwing a ball for Kelly. She is a frequent contributor to the Huffington Post.

Her other award winning books include:

Cedar Bay Cozy Mystery Series
Kelly's Koffee Shop, Murder at Jade Cove, White Cloud Retreat, Marriage and Murder, Murder in the Pearl District, Murder in Calico Gold, Murder at the Cooking School, Murder in Cuba

Liz Lucas Cozy Mystery Series
Murder in Cottage #6, Murder & Brandy Boy, The Death Card, Murder at The Bed & Breakfast

High Desert Cozy Mystery Series
Murder & The Monkey Band, Murder & The Secret Cave

Coyote Series
Blue Coyote Motel, Coyote in Provence, Cornered Coyote

Website: www.dianneharman.com
Blog: www.dianneharman.com/blog
Email: dianne@dianneharman.com

Newsletter
If you would like to be notified of her latest releases please go to www.dianneharman.com and sign up for her newsletter.

CPSIA information can be obtained
at www.ICGtesting.com
Printed in the USA
BVHW03s2138200618
519613BV00001B/41/P